"You just verified something for me."

"What's that?"

"You are naughty."

She laughed again. "Only at times."

"We'll see about that."

Mia wasn't given time to ponder Kenyon's cryptic statement—she found herself in his arms again and carried into the en suite bath. There was a soaking tub set into a raised platform and a shower enclosure with two showerheads.

Anchoring her arms under his shoulders, she pressed her breasts to his chest when he lowered her feet to the shower floor. The area between her legs was wet, throbbing. Her craving for Kenyon surpassed anything she'd ever felt and didn't want to feel again. She sucked in her breath when a stream of cold water flowed over her head before Kenyon adjusted the temperature.

"It is warm enough now?"

Mia nodded. She wanted to tell him she was on fire, that she needed him inside her to extinguish the flame. "Yes-s-s."

Books by Rochelle Alers

Kimani Romance

Bittersweet Love
Sweet Deception
Sweet Dreams
Twice the Temptation
Sweet Persuasions
Sweet Destiny

ROCHELLE ALERS

has been hailed by readers and booksellers alike as one of today's most prolific and popular African-American authors of romance and women's fiction.

With more than sixty titles and nearly two million copies of her novels in print, Ms. Alers is a regular on the Waldenbooks, Borders and *Essence* bestseller lists, is regularly chosen by Black Expressions Book Club and has been the recipient of numerous awards, including a Gold Pen Award, an Emma Award, a Vivian Stephens Award for Excellence in Romance Writing, an *RT Book Reviews* Career Achievement Award and a Zora Neale Hurston Literary Award.

Ms. Alers is a member of the Iota Theta Zeta chapter of Zeta Phi Beta Sorority, Inc., and her interests include gourmet cooking and traveling. She has traveled to Europe and countries in North, South and Central America. Her future travel plans include visits to Hong Kong and New Zealand. Ms. Alers is also accomplished in knitting, crocheting and needlepoint. She is currently taking instruction in the art of hand quilting.

Oliver, a toy Yorkshire terrier, has become the newest addition to her family. When he's not barking at passing school buses, the tiny dog can be found sleeping on her lap while she spends hours in front of the computer.

A full-time writer, Ms. Alers lives in a charming hamlet on Long Island.

Sweet Destiny

ROCHELLE ALERS

KIMANI ROMANCE

Blessed are the meek, for they will inherit the land.
—*Matthew* 5:5

To my editor, Evette Porter—
thanks for the encouragement, chats and the laughs
as we continue this incredible journey together.

KIMANI PRESS™

Recycling programs for this product may not exist in your area.

ISBN-13: 978-0-373-86216-0

SWEET DESTINY

www.kimanipress.com

Printed in U.S.A.

Dear Reader,

Welcome to the second of a two-book Eaton summer wedding series. This time it is Dr. Mia Eaton's turn to walk down the aisle.

I set *Sweet Destiny* in West Virginia's Mingo County to offer you a glimpse into a slower, more humble way of life. Dallas born and bred, Mia does not know what to expect when she accepts a position as a public health doctor in a region of Appalachia described as "rich yet poor, exploited yet underdeveloped, scarred yet beautiful." This also describes Kenyon Chandler—a man who views pampered, snobby Mia as geographically undesirable until she proves she has the determination and resolve to become the first Eaton to put down roots in the Mountain State.

Look for Dr. Levi Eaton's *Sweet Southern Nights* in early 2012, when he meets a true Southern belle living a double life. Tempers flare, sparks fly and the only happily-ever-after Angela Chase is certain of is what she reads in her romance novels.

Read, love and read romance.

Rochelle Alers

www.rochellealers.org
ralersbooks@aol.com

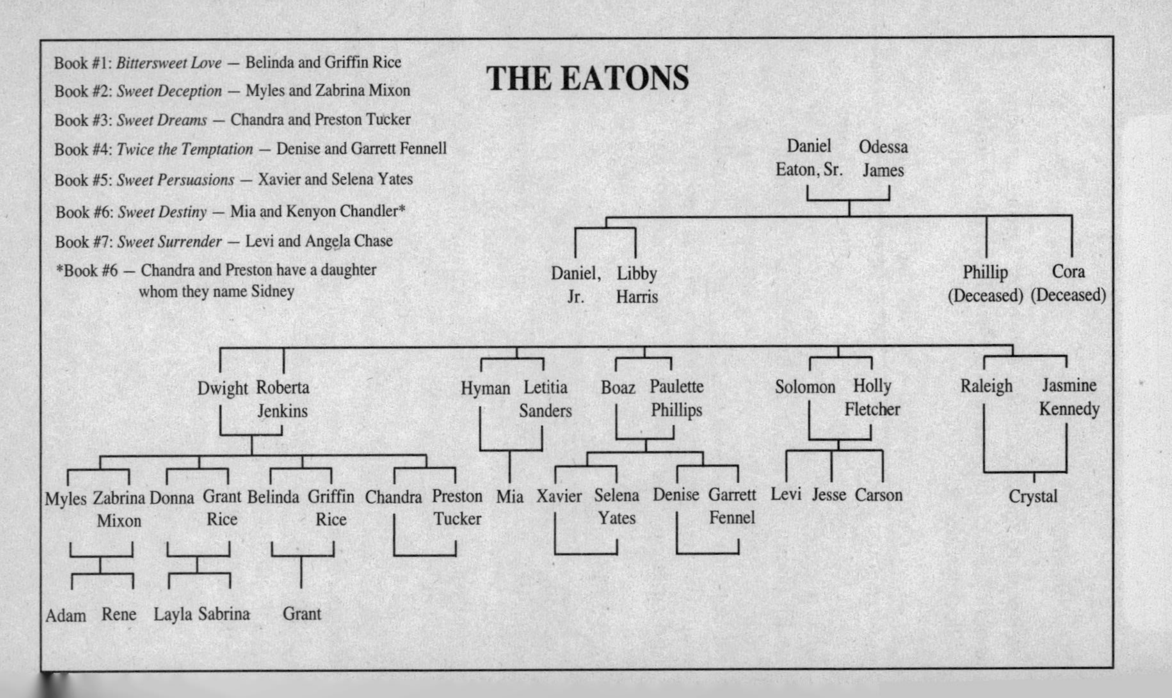

Book #1: *Bittersweet Love* — Belinda and Griffin Rice
Book #2: *Sweet Deception* — Myles and Zabrina Mixon
Book #3: *Sweet Dreams* — Chandra and Preston Tucker
Book #4: *Twice the Temptation* — Denise and Garrett Fennell
Book #5: *Sweet Persuasions* — Xavier and Selena Yates
Book #6: *Sweet Destiny* — Mia and Kenyon Chandler*
Book #7: *Sweet Surrender* — Levi and Angela Chase
*Book #6 — Chandra and Preston have a daughter whom they name Sidney
THE EATONS
Daniel Eaton, Sr.
Odessa James
Daniel, Jr.
Libby Harris
Phillip (Deceased)
Cora (Deceased)
Dwight
Roberta Jenkins
Hyman
Letitia Sanders
Boaz
Paulette Phillips
Solomon
Holly Fletcher
Raleigh
Jasmine Kennedy
Myles
Zabrina Mixon
Donna
Grant Rice
Belinda
Griffin Rice
Chandra
Preston Tucker
Mia
Xavier
Selena Yates
Denise
Garrett Fennel
Levi
Jesse
Carson
Crystal
Adam
Rene
Layla
Sabrina
Grant

Chapter 1

"Are you sure you're all right?" Mia Eaton asked a very pregnant Chandra Eaton-Tucker, when she noticed her cousin fidgeting restlessly on the window seat.

With one hand resting on her swollen belly and the other at the small of her back, Chandra exhaled audibly. "I'm good. It was just another contraction."

Mia gave Chandra a look that made her cousin sit up straight. "How close are your contractions?"

"Not close at all. I am not in labor, Dr. Eaton," Chandra said, as she pressed the back of her hand to her forehead. "Please give me a few minutes to get myself together."

"Don't..." The door to the bedroom opened as the sound of voices interrupted Mia.

Denise Eaton swept into the room wearing a diaphanous wedding dress made of yards of white silk and satin, trailed by the bride's cousin Belinda Rice, in a black silk-chiffon, Regency-inspired, floor-length gown.

It was New Year's Eve, just four hours before the clock struck midnight, and close to a hundred people, including family and friends of the bride and groom, had gathered in the ballroom of a palatial Philadelphia colonial to witness the exchange of vows between Denise Eaton and Garrett Fennell. The bride had chosen her cousins Chandra, Belinda and Mia as her attendants. The groom's stepfather, half brother and a close business associate were Garrett's groomsmen.

Mia watched Denise as she lifted the skirt to her gown to reveal a pair of hand-embroidered antique shoes. The heels of the bride's shoes dug deeply into the carpet. A profusion of miniature white roses pinned in her tightly curled hair took the place of a veil. With a slight lift of Chandra's chin, the motion barely perceptible to the others in the room, Mia turned and walked toward the door as Denise and Belinda followed.

"Please, Mia, don't tell me Chandra's going to push that baby out before the ceremony." Denise's expression had changed from shock to concern.

Mia smiled, shaking her head. "She's not going to have her baby. But she is in some discomfort. I know she isn't going to want me to examine her, but maybe you can ask my dad to check on her." Mia Eaton had followed in her father's footsteps and graduated from medical school. But unlike Dr. Hyman Eaton, whose specialty was obstetrics and gynecology, she had opted for family medicine like her uncle Dwight.

One of the Eaton family's long-standing traditions was that you either went into medicine, law or education. But the occupational landscape had changed for the current generation of Eatons.

Lately it seemed as if there was either an Eaton wedding or birth several times a year. Mia had attended the weddings of Belinda and Griffin Rice, Myles and Zabrina Mixon, and Chandra and Preston Tucker. Now she was part of the bridal party of Denise and Garrett Fennell. Another generation of Eatons had arrived with the birth of Grant Rice II and his cousins Layla and Sabrina, who were being raised by their aunt and uncle, Belinda and Griffin; there were also Myles and Zabrina's 10-year-old son, Adam, and their infant daughter, Renee Eaton. And in about another month Chandra was expected to give birth. She and her husband had decided that they didn't want to know the sex of the baby beforehand. Mia's plans, however, did not include marriage or children for at least for five or six years. She'd completed her internship, passed her medical boards and was now focused on her residency.

Belinda's gaze shifted from her sister Chandra to her cousin. "You stay here, Denise. After all, you're the bride and people shouldn't see you before the ceremony. I'll go and get Uncle Hyman."

Denise nodded. When she'd asked Chandra to be her matron of honor, she knew Chandra was pregnant. However the baby wasn't expected until mid-to-late January. "Okay," she said. "I'll wait here."

Mia and Denise sat on either side of Chandra, holding her hand. The resemblance between the three cousins was remarkable. They were undeniably Eaton women, having inherited their rich golden-brown coloring and thick curly hair from their paternal grandmother, Libby Harris-Eaton.

Denise looked at Mia. "I can't believe you're serious about doing your residency in West Virginia instead of Texas."

A smile parted her lips. "Believe it, cousin. Doctors are as scarce as hen's teeth in the area where I plan to practice."

"Had you considered becoming a small-town doctor before we went to Matewan for my brother's wedding?" Denise's brother Xavier Eaton had married Selena Yates in Charleston, South Carolina, after a whirlwind romance. The two had repeated their vows in a West Virginia church overflowing with members of the Eaton and Yates families. After the ceremony, everyone retreated to a barn that had been transformed into an elegant setting with tiny white lights, bales of hay and cornstalks for a festive Thanksgiving dinner reception. The food, music and down-home atmosphere turned into a party that went on well into the early morning hours.

"No," Mia said truthfully. "At Xavier's reception, I overhead someone at my table talk about having to drive more than twenty miles to the nearest hospital just to have some blood work done because the local doctor had moved away. Driving forty miles round-trip to have blood drawn when it can be done in a doctor's office and sent off to a lab is ridiculous in this day and age, Dee. That's when I decided to stay an extra week and check out whether my medical training could best be utilized in rural West Virginia."

Mia had gone online and inquired about employment opportunities for doctors on West Virginia's Department of Health and Human Services website. And before the end of the week, she had an interview. When she was told that the only doctor in the small town of Jonesburg was semiretired, she decided to accept an offer to assist the elderly family physician.

A hint of a smile tilted the corners of Denise's generous mouth. "So, my high-maintenance cousin is going to trade in her designer threads for flannel and work boots to become a small-town doctor."

"That's a small sacrifice when compared to offering

people, many of whom are living at or below the poverty line, adequate medical care."

Denise sobered. "You've changed, Mia."

"In what way?" she asked.

A beat passed and Chandra opened her eyes. "We used to call you Little Miss Tish."

Mia blinked and then went completely still, holding her breath until she felt her chest tightly constrict. Her eyes narrowed as she was forced to breathe. "Are you saying I *act* like my mother did?"

Letitia Sanders-Eaton had never gotten along with her in-laws, and the feeling was mutual. There were years when Mia didn't see her Philadelphia cousins because Tish Eaton thought they were too boorish for her taste. She hadn't agreed with her mother's assessment of the rest of the Eatons, so when she'd applied and was accepted at a number of colleges, Mia decided to attend the University of Pennsylvania so that she would be close to her relatives. Despite promising her father that she would attend his alma mater, Texas Southwestern, for medical school, she'd exercised her newfound independence even more and attended Baylor College of Medicine in Houston.

She gave the soon-to-be mother a sidelong glance. "That's cold, Chandra."

"You do act a little snobby at times," Denise added, agreeing with Chandra.

"I am not a snob!"

Chandra laughed, resting a hand over her protruding belly, which was covered by the billowy skirt of the black silk chiffon gown. "You remind me of Nixon when he said 'I am not a crook.'" She affected a gruff-sounding voice reminiscent of the former president that had Denise and Mia laughing uncontrollably.

Mia released Chandra's hand. "You must be feeling a lot

better." She smoothed the skirt of her empire-waist gown. In keeping with the New Year's Eve holiday theme, Denise Eaton had decided on a black-and-white color scheme for her wedding. All of the bridesmaids wore black dresses, and Denise wore a black satin sash around the waistline of her white gown.

Chandra winked at Denise as she rose from the window seat. "If you're ready to get married, then I'm ready to waddle across the ballroom as your matron of honor." She was on her feet by the time there was a knock at the door and two tuxedo-clad middle-aged men entered the bedroom. "It's okay. I'm all right," she said, as doctors Hyman and Dwight Eaton approached.

Hyman looked closely at his niece. "Are saying you're all right because you don't want me to examine you, or are you really all right?"

Chandra pressed her hands together, as the overhead fixture refracted the brilliant blue-and-white prisms of light that bounced off the diamonds on her left hand. "Yes, I am really all right. Can we please do this so I can sit down?"

Denise smiled at her attendants. "Okay ladies. Let's do this."

The four women picked up the beautiful bouquets that lined the padded bench at the foot of the queen-size bed in Denise's childhood bedroom.

Mia sat at the bridal table, nodding and smiling as the hands on the wristwatch of the man sitting on her right inched closer to one in the morning. Although she didn't get to see her Pennsylvania relatives as much as she'd liked, she'd always managed to stay abreast of family news, since Denise, Chandra or Belinda would occasionally email her with the latest gossip.

She was more than a bit shocked to learn that Trey Chambers Jr. was really Garrett Fennell's half brother. The last she'd heard was that Rhett and Trey had had a falling out over Denise, but that was before Rhett was aware that he and Trey had the same father.

Trey Chambers cast a sidelong glance at the woman with the close-cropped, curly black hair who'd been his partner in the wedding party. She was stunning—tall and slender, with curves in all the right places. Trey saw Mia as more the high-fashion model type than a doctor. Her large dark, wide-set eyes didn't look at him, but through him. It was as if she could see through the slick veneer he'd affected over the years to get women into bed. It'd worked on most women, but not with Mia Eaton. And he'd certainly tried and failed several times to get her number.

His gaze lingered on her delicate profile, with lips so tempting that he was forced to look away. "Are you certain you don't want me to get you something to drink?" he asked in a quiet tone.

Mia forced a smile. "I'm very certain," she said. Rising from the table, she pushed back her chair. "Please excuse me." She had to leave to change out of the gown and into clothes suitable for traveling.

After the reception, Mia, Xavier and his wife, Selena, were planning to fly to Kentucky and then travel on to Matewan, West Virginia, where the newlyweds would spend a week with her family before returning to South Carolina. Xavier had reserved a car that would take her and his wife to a regional airport for a nonstop flight to Pikesville, Kentucky. Mia planned to stay overnight with the Yates', then drive eighteen miles south to Jonesburg to meet the local physician, Dr. Millard Lyman, and settle into her new place. She'd packed enough to last a week, hoping the rest of her luggage filled with clothes and other items she would need to set up her apartment would arrive in West Virginia as planned.

Before leaving the reception, Mia nodded to her father as he spun her mother around the ballroom dance floor. Her relationship with her mother, Leticia, had become somewhat strained, since her mother refused to accept the fact that she wanted to become a country doctor instead of setting up her own practice in Dallas.

Twenty minutes after retreating to Denise's bedroom, Mia walked out with a leather tote containing her ticket and a carry-on bag. Dressed in jeans, Doc Martens, an Irish-knit pullover sweater and ski jacket, she left the house through a rear entrance.

The driver sitting behind the wheel of a town car got out and opened the rear door upon her approach. He touched the shiny bill of his cap before he took her bags. "Mr. and Mrs. Eaton are on their way."

Mia nodded, ducking her head as she got into the limo. She was dog-tired—exhausted. After working a double shift, her flight had arrived in Philadelphia just hours before the wedding rehearsal, followed by the rehearsal dinner at a popular restaurant.

The next morning was spent at a full-service beauty salon and spa. A facial, massage, waxing, manicure and pedicure, followed by a midday snack and then hair and makeup, had left her more out of sorts than relaxed. Much to her mother's chagrin, she'd opted to have her hair styled in a low-maintenance pixie cut. The shortened strands would save valuable time because she wouldn't have to set and blow-dry her hair.

Settling back on the leather seat, she closed her eyes. Mia stirred when she felt Selena and Xavier join her in the rear of the limousine, but she didn't open her eyes. She was wide awake, however, by the time they arrived at the regional airport and went through security. Almost as soon as she fastened her seat belt, she fell asleep again before takeoff.

"We're here."

Mia's eyelids fluttered as she tried to get her bearings. They were on the ground, and the small aircraft was taxiing to the gate at the small terminal. She smiled at Selena Yates-Eaton, owner of Sweet Persuasions, a Charleston, South Carolina pastry shop. The pastry chef had made the most beautiful wedding cake for her sister-in-law. The detailed flowers on the cake matched those in Denise's wedding bouquet.

Stretching her body like a cat, she rolled her head from side to side. "How long will it take to get to your hometown?"

Selena smiled, scrunching up her nose. "It'll be long enough for you to take another power nap."

Mia massaged the back of her neck. "I don't think I'll ever catch up when it comes to sleep."

"Treating patients in Mingo County will be a lot different than seeing those in a big city. I'm not saying you won't have your share of patients with health problems, but it will mostly be sick kids and their mothers. Most men don't put much stock in seeing a doctor unless it's absolutely necessary. Speaking of men, I'd better turn on my cell phone and see if my dad called. He said he would come to pick us up."

Mia liked her cousin's wife. Although she found Selena friendly, Selena also possessed a certain shyness that Mia found endearing. And, she knew Selena had to be quite special if Xavier had been willing to give up bachelorhood. Mia had lost count of the number of women who'd asked her to introduce them to the one-time career military officer. But she usually told them he was involved with another woman, to avoid any hurt feelings. Most of her med school classmates were looking for husbands, and what they hadn't known about Xavier was that he wasn't the marrying kind—until now.

The aircraft had come to a complete stop and the seat-belt light was extinguished. Xavier unsnapped his seat belt and moved toward the seat facing Mia's. He smiled. "Feeling better?"

She returned his smile. "Like a new woman." Mia felt better than she had in days. The flight was just long enough for her to get a little shut-eye.

Xavier patted her head as he'd done when they were younger. "You'll get to sleep in late, because Selena's folks usually stay up late on New Year's Eve and then sit down to celebrate later in the afternoon with a traditional Southern dinner."

"Daddy isn't going to pick us up," Selena said, listening to her father's voice-mail message.

Xavier looked at his wife. With her youthful appearance she looked like she was still in high school. "Let's hope we can rent a car."

Selena shook her head. "Kenyon's coming to pick us up." She stared at Mia, remembering Kenyon's remark at her wedding reception. He thought Mia was pretty, but he also thought that she was stuck-up. And she was looking forward to seeing the sheriff of Jonesburg's reaction when he was formally introduced to Dr. Mia Eaton, the town's new doctor.

Mia waited with the others in the biting cold January night, while their luggage was unloaded from the plane's cargo compartment and left on the tarmac for passengers to retrieve. She smiled. There was no moving sidewalk, no elevator, no escalator or monorail to the baggage claim area. It was de-board the plane and pick up your bags. Xavier grasped the handle to Mia's luggage, while shouldering his own. Minutes later they walked into a warm terminal. There were at least a dozen people waiting for arriving passengers, hugging and kissing their loved ones, greeting one another for the New Year.

Kenyon Chandler saw his cousin, her husband and a woman he was sure he'd never see again. It had been a little more than a month, but he'd remembered everything about her as if it had been minutes before. Taking long, smooth strides, he closed the distance between himself and the trio.

He noticed the difference in Mia Eaton immediately. She'd cut her hair, the style accentuating her incredibly beautiful face. He felt the full force of her gaze, meeting and fusing with his. The recognition was barely perceptible, but she'd lifted her chin, staring at him along the length of her delicate nose. He was unsure whether she was staring at him with aloofness or icy disdain.

Reluctantly, he pulled his eyes away from the tall woman in a pair of jeans that hugged her hips and long legs like a second skin, and he smiled at Selena. "Happy New Year, cuz." Bending his head, he kissed her cheek.

Looping her arms around Kenyon's neck, Selena pressed a kiss to his smooth jaw. "Same to you. What's up with my dad?"

"He had a little too much holiday libation," Kenyon whispered in her ear. Reaching up, he eased her arms from around his neck and extended a hand to Xavier. "Welcome back."

Xavier shook his hand, slapping Kenyon's shoulder. "Thank you. I don't know if you were ever formally introduced to my cousin at the wedding." Turning slightly, he reached for Mia's free hand, pulling her to his side. "Mia, this is Kenyon Chandler. Kenyon, Mia Eaton. She's going to be Jonesburg's new doctor."

The expression on Kenyon's face spoke volumes. As sheriff of Jonesburg he hadn't been informed by the mayor or any of the trustees that they were getting a new doctor. Recovering quickly, he offered Mia his hand. "Even though we're in Kentucky, I'd like to be the first one to extend a warm welcome to Jonesburg, West Virginia."

Mia stared at the large hand as if it were a venomous reptile. Seconds later her hand disappeared into his warm grasp. She detected calluses on the palm, which told her Kenyon was no stranger to hard work. She felt as if she were lost in a fog when she stared into a pair of large, deep-set dark gray eyes ringed by long, thick black lashes. His eyes were a startling contrast to his dark brown coloring.

"Thank you so much." Mia's smile and voice was filled with sincerity.

Kenyon reached for her luggage and Selena's carry-on. "I'm parked outside." Turning on his heels, he led the way out of the terminal to the parking lot. Pressing a button on a remote device he started up a dark blue SUV with West Virginia license plates. A placard in the windshield identified him as Mingo County law enforcement. He opened the passenger-side door. "Mia, you can ride up front with me. That way you can tell me why you decided to practice medicine in Appalachia instead of in the big city."

Mia went completely still. Had she heard him right? Was there a hint of derisiveness in Kenyon's voice? She squared her shoulders. Her eyes moved slowly over the features under the wide-brim, Western-style black hat. Despite her annoyance she had to admit he was drop-dead gorgeous. When he leaned forward and lowered his impressive height, he still eclipsed Mia, who was five-ten, by another four or five inches.

"Does it really matter why I'm here? Shouldn't it be more about addressing the medical needs of the people in this region?"

"It's just that I need to know a little something about the folks who hang out in my town."

"Hang out! What makes you think I'm here to hang—"

"We'll talk later," Kenyon interrupted. "It's cold and late, and the weather folks are predicting snow. So let's go before the roads get too slippery."

Mia clenched her teeth to stop the verbal tirade poised on the tip of her tongue. Kenyon was right. It was late, and the night air was biting and raw. There was also a fog in the air that hinted of precipitation. She let the obnoxious man cup her elbow as she hoisted herself onto the front seat of the SUV. She stared out the windshield as the door closed with a solid thud. The heat flowing through the vehicle's vents wrapped around her like a blanket, pulling her into a cocoon of warmth and relaxation. Her mother had been disappointed in her decision to leave Dallas, and Kenyon Chandler was suspicious because she'd chosen to practice medicine in Appalachia.

Mia understood her mother's attitude, but what she couldn't fathom was Kenyon's skepticism. Maybe it didn't matter to him that someone had to drive twenty miles one way for a procedure that could have been done in a doctor's office, saving the patient time *and* money. He'd mentioned *his town,* and she wondered if he was oblivious to the medical needs of its residents. It wasn't as if they lived in a large urban area, or even a suburb where there was easy access to hospitals and medical clinics. She'd researched the demographics of Jonesburg, and the per capita income for the town was depressing. She'd grown up with girls who spent more money on clothes, makeup and perfume in a year than the median income for Jonesburg's households.

Nothing her mother or Kenyon had said could dampen her enthusiasm for practicing medicine alongside a doctor with nearly forty years of experience. She'd come to West Virginia to work with Dr. Lyman and eventually take over his practice once he retired.

Chapter 2

Mia didn't fall asleep, preferring instead to stare out the side window at the surrounding landscape. Xavier and Selena had fallen asleep in the rear seat within minutes of getting into the Yukon SUV.

Kenyon had tuned the vehicle's radio to a station that featured blues music as sad as it was haunting. Music her mother said was played in juke joints throughout the South—music law-abiding and churchgoing folks would never listen to.

A slight smile softened her mouth when a husky-throated woman, accompanied by a harmonica and guitar, sang about loving her no-account, cheating lover. And no matter how many women he'd fooled with, she loved him because he was the only man who made her feel like a real live woman, according to the lyrics.

"She's a fool," Mia mumbled between clenched teeth.

"Is she a fool for loving her man, or a fool for putting up with his cheating?"

She turned and stared at Kenyon. He'd removed his hat and she was able to see all of his face. Dark, short-cropped hair hugged his well-shaped head like a cap. It was the first thing he'd said in more than forty minutes, and she chided herself for voicing her thoughts aloud.

"Both. There's no reason why a woman should have to put up with a cheating man."

"Why do you think they do?"

The seconds ticked before she said, "Low self-esteem. I believe women who put up with cheating men love the men more than they love themselves, and for me that's a no-no."

Kenyon drummed his fingers on the steering wheel, keeping rhythm with the music flowing through the sound system. That single statement told him all he wanted or needed to know about Mia. If or when it came to a relationship, she would be unforgiving.

"You like blues?" Kenyon had asked yet another question, deftly changing the topic.

"Some."

"Which do you prefer?"

Her eyebrows lifted. "I thought they were all the same."

Kenyon took his eyes off the narrow unlit road for a second, his gaze caressing Mia's face as she stared directly at him. "There's Delta blues, Chicago and Detroit blues."

"I like B. B. King."

"Good Mississippi bluesman."

"What about Eric Clapton?"

Kenyon smiled, and attractive lines fanned out around his luminous eyes. "Another fine bluesman, albeit from across the pond."

Mia noticed the harsh edge in Kenyon's voice was missing. Could it be he wasn't *that* resentful of her moving into his town? "Should I assume you are the law in Jonesburg?"

The vocalist had stopped, and there was only the sound of harmonica playing, the haunting beats keeping tempo with the sound of tires slapping the roadway. She thought he hadn't heard her, so Mia shifted again to stare out the side window. It was beginning to snow. Tiny flakes fluttered from a sky too dark to see, landing on the asphalt roadway. Naked tree branches along the highway broke up the occasional flecks of light that shone through the windows of those who were still in the partying mood or had left the lights on for latecomers.

They crossed the state line from Kentucky into West Virginia, and if it hadn't been for the highway marker Mia would not have been able to discern one state from the other. She was in mining country, where the hills rose and fell, and where great mounds of earth were stripped for their rich mineral deposits.

"Yes, I am the sheriff of Jonesburg."

It had been a full two minutes since Mia had asked the question—so long that she thought Kenyon hadn't heard it or he had decided not to answer.

She turned to look at him again. He and Selena were cousins, but the only physical resemblance they shared was in their coloring, and she wondered if perhaps they were related by marriage. "How long have you been in office?"

"Why do you want to know?"

"If I'm going to live in Jonesburg, then I believe I should know something about the people who live there." She'd turned the tables, repeating what he'd said to her.

Kenyon decelerated as he maneuvered around a sharp curve in the road. The snow was coming down harder. "How long do you plan to live in Jonesburg? Two months?"

"Try two years," she countered. "I have another two years before I complete my residency."

"What happens after you complete your residency?"

"You're asking a lot of questions, Sheriff Chandler. If you suspect I have some ulterior motive, then I suggest you have me investigated. That shouldn't be too difficult. I'll even help you out. My name is Mia Isabel Eaton. I was born in Dallas, Texas, on June—"

"There's no need for you to be facetious, Mia," Kenyon interrupted.

"I'm not being facetious, Kenyon. My living in Jonesburg serves two purposes—completing my residency and helping a semiretired doctor who can no longer make house calls."

A muscle twitched in Kenyon's jaw. The image of the woman he'd observed at Selena's wedding reception was imprinted in his mind like a permanent tattoo. Her hair had been brushed off her face and knotted loosely on the nape of her neck with jeweled hairpins that matched the large diamond studs in her earlobes. She'd worn a one-shouldered dress in a shade that was the exact color of the pumpkins in the centerpieces on each table. She had on snakeskin stilettos in various colors of yellow, red, orange and brown, which added at least four inches to her statuesque figure. She even towered over some of the men in attendance.

A woman's height was never an issue with Kenyon. At fourteen he was just shy of the six-foot mark, and by the time he'd turned eighteen he stood six-four and his body had filled out where his ribs were no longer visible. By the time he received his official discharge from the Air Force he'd tipped the scales at 220 pounds.

He would've asked Mia to dance but didn't, even after Selena had offered to introduce him to her. The woman with the beautiful face and perfect body, wearing priceless jewelry and haute couture, was a snob, and she hadn't bothered to hide her disdain for his folk. And for as long as he'd stared at her—not once had she smiled or approached anyone other than *her* relatives. It had appeared as if the talk about the joining of two families didn't apply to her.

Now, four weeks later, she had returned to Mingo County, this time to live. Kenyon wanted to warn Mia that her haughty manner would not endear her to the people who didn't cotton to folks who put on airs.

Mia was right—he had asked a lot of questions, but it been years since someone had come to Jonesburg to live. Most times it was people moving out because they'd either tired of living in a small town where everyone knew everyone *and* their business, or they were offered better employment opportunities elsewhere. For those living in towns like Jonesburg, generations became miners because their fathers, grandfathers, great-grandfathers and great-great-grandfathers were coal miners.

He'd decided not to ask any more questions and instead watched her closely. Six months. That was how much time he'd give Mia before she packed up and returned to the pampered life she'd left behind.

The drive to Matewan took Kenyon twice as long as it would have if it hadn't been snowing. He'd had to slow down because the snow was falling at a rate of two inches an hour, but it was also wet and heavy. The sound of branches breaking under the weight of the frozen precipitation resounded like gunfire in the stillness of the night. Heavyweight snow also meant loss of power when electrical wires snapped, plunging homes and businesses into darkness until utility crews could get to the region to repair them.

Downshifting, he turned off the county road and onto a local one leading to the house where his grandmother lived with his aunt and uncle. His mother had tried to get her mother to come and live with her, but Lily Yates refused to move out of the converted garage Kenyon and his uncle had renovated into a one-bedroom apartment after her husband passed away.

He maneuvered into the carport next to a late-model sport utility vehicle with Texas plates. The silver Volvo hadn't been there when he'd left for the airport. Apparently Mia had arranged for her vehicle to be delivered to coincide with her arrival. Kenyon had to admire her for planning ahead. What he still found disturbing was that he hadn't been informed that Dr. Lyman would have a partner.

He turned off the radio and the engine. "Don't move. I'll help you down." Mia had unsnapped her seat belt.

Mia waited for Kenyon to get out, come around and open her door. He extended his arms and she slid off the seat, her arms going around his neck as he held her aloft for several seconds before her boots sank into a mound of drifting snow.

She smiled. "Thank you."

A beat passed as he stared at her mouth. Even her smile was sensual. "You're welcome. Go inside the house where it's warm."

Mia hesitated. "Aren't you going to unlock the door?"

"It's probably unlocked." Kenyon motioned with his head. "Go! Now, before you catch a chill."

Rolling her eyes and carefully putting one foot in front of the other to keep from falling, she walked tentatively up the four steps leading to the porch. She'd left the Lone Star State for the City of Brotherly Love, and then went onto the Mountain State, where the temperatures ranged from the low sixties to below freezing. But Mia was totally unprepared for the snow and biting wind that seemed to search through layers of clothing, chilling her to the bone.

The large farmhouse had a wraparound porch; electric candles lit the many windows, and a large, live pine wreath festooned with tiny glazed ceramic apples, acorns and holly berries was attached to the front door. Mia turned the knob and the door opened. She couldn't believe people actually went to bed without locking their doors at night. She'd grown up where not only were doors locked at all times, but the house and property was wired and monitored by cameras and a 24/7 security company. She knew it would take her a while to adjust to living and working in a small town.

Stepping onto a thick coir mat, Mia stomped the snow off the soles of her boots before she leaned over to unlace them. She left the Doc Martens on a rag rug lined with boots and shoes. Two dimly lit hurricane lamps on either end of a long wooden table revealed a highly polished walnut floor. Her gaze shifted to the smoldering stone fireplace facing her, and the sweet smell of burning kindling mingled with a scent she recognized as pine. She walked into the living room, smiling. A live pine tree decorated in tiny white lights was positioned near the arched entryway to the dining room. The miniature lights were the same as those that had decorated the barn where Xavier and Selena held their wedding reception. However, these blinked off and on like twinkling stars.

Selena, who'd also removed her shoes, joined her in the living room. "If you follow me I'll show you where you'll sleep. I'm giving you my old room, because it's on the top floor and soundproof. That way you can sleep as late as you want and not hear whatever ruckus is going on down here."

Mia followed Selena as she mounted the staircase, which had a massive mahogany banister and carved newel posts. She couldn't wait until daylight to see the magnificent beauty of the wood in the farmhouse. Their sock-covered feet were silent as they climbed the staircase from the first to the third floor. Standing on the landing, she saw there were three doors.

Selena opened one door, reached in and flicked on a switch, and the room where she'd spent her childhood was flooded with soft light from a ceiling fan. She stood to one side as Mia walked in, her eyes taking in everything in what had at one time been her sanctuary.

"Awesome, isn't it?"

Mia nodded numbly. A four-poster bed, draped in a gossamer fabric, was positioned in an alcove facing another recessed area with a massive armoire fashioned out of the same dark mahogany wood. A window seat running the width of the room could easily accommodate six people. The grate in a stone fireplace, similar to the one in the living room, held a supply of firewood. A large bronze bucket was filled with wood and kindling. Someone hadn't bothered to close the screen.

"It's incredible," she said, when she found her voice. "Who designed this room?"

"My grandfather. He built this house and most of the furniture in it. If he hadn't been a carpenter or furniture maker he would have become a coal miner. Speaking of furniture, there's a TV and a collection of DVDs in the armoire."

"Do you have relatives who are or were miners?" Mia asked.

Selena nodded. "There are several generations of miners on my grandmother's side of the family. Grandma Lily lost two brothers and an uncle in an explosion, and she vowed that none of her children would ever work in a mine. She did everything, taking in wash, making and selling quilts and even babysitting to put away enough money to send my father and aunt to college. Dad majored in criminal justice and he's now sheriff of Matewan, and

Kenyon's mother is an expert when it comes to textile designs. Aunt Sylvia's weaving and quilts are exhibited in the American Folk Art Museum in New York City, and she has donated a collection of quilts to the Textile Heritage Museum in Burlington, North Carolina. Thankfully, my paternal grandfather was the last one to work as a coal miner."

Mia smiled. One of her questions had been answered. Selena's father and Kenyon's mother were siblings. There were a few more questions Mia wanted to ask, but she decided it would be impolite to pry. She didn't know what it was about Kenyon that elicited more than a passing interest. Although he hadn't worn a ring, she didn't know if he was married, single or committed to someone. And, if he was committed then the woman could count herself lucky to have snared such a gorgeous male specimen.

The object of her musings chose that moment to walk into the bedroom carrying her luggage. He'd removed his jacket, and the long-sleeved waffle-weave shirt couldn't conceal the power in his upper body. Her eyes went to the silver buckle on his belt, but she wasn't close enough to read the inscription on the ornate piece.

"Thank you for bringing up my bags."

Kenyon nodded, and then set the tote and Pullman on the floor next to the door. "If you've made plans to go to Jonesburg tomorrow, then scrap them."

A slight frown appeared between Mia's eyes. "Why?"

"I just got an email that because of blizzard conditions the governor has declared a snow emergency for Mingo, McDowell and Wyoming counties. Only emergency vehicles carrying essential personnel will be permitted on the roads."

Mia folded her arms under her breasts. "Can't I ride along with you? Dr. Lyman is expecting me Monday."

"No, you can't ride along with me, because I'm staying here until the road is clear."

"But…but aren't you the sheriff?"

A slow smile spread across Kenyon's face, the expression making him even more appealing. "I do have deputies who are more than capable of filling in for me. Once the roads are plowed I will give you a police escort to Jonesburg."

Mia lowered her arms. "I suppose I don't have much of a choice, do I?"

"No, you don't."

Selena glanced at her watch. "I don't know about you two, but I'm going to try and get at least four hours of sleep before I have to get up and start baking. Mia, you're a guest, so you can sleep in as late as you want."

Mia wanted to tell Selena she doubted if she was going to get up late because she'd slept during the flight from Philadelphia to Pikesville. "I'll see you in the morning."

"It's already morning," Kenyon said, reminding her that it was after four in the morning.

Selena took Kenyon's arm. "Let's go, wise guy. Mia, the bathroom is the middle door in the landing."

"Thanks."

"There's no need to thank me. After all, we are family."

After all, we are family. The five words stayed with Mia as she opened her luggage to retrieve a nightgown and grooming supplies. Selena may have considered her family, but she doubted whether Kenyon did. There was no doubt he thought of her as an outsider, an interloper who should've stayed in the big city. Well, it didn't matter what he thought or how he viewed her, she wasn't going anywhere. She'd come to Mingo County to practice medicine and no one—and that included the law—would stop her from fulfilling her commitment to give the residents of Jonesburg the best care she could provide.

Even though the attic bedroom was warm, the lace-trimmed silk garment was definitely not warm enough for West Virginia's winter. It seemed as if she would have to trade in Victoria's Secret for L.L. Bean. She took out a matching robe, placing the garments on the foot of the large bed. Sleeping in the bed draped with yards of fabric must have made Selena feel like a princess.

Walking out of the bedroom with the quilted pouch filled with toiletries, Mia opened the door to the bathroom. A light came on automatically when the door opened. The space was small, but homey. A claw-foot bathtub, with a shower attachment, pedestal sink and a commode harkened back to a bygone era. A bleached pine table cradled an assortment of towels, cloths and bottles of shampoo, conditioner and bath gel.

She turned on the faucets, and added a dollop of bath gel under the running water, and within seconds the distinctive scent of lavender filled the space. Mia brushed her teeth and cleansed her face, rinsing it with cold water, before she stripped off her clothes and stepped into the bathtub. A soft moan escaped her parted lips as she sank lower in the warm water. It was the perfect way to end what had become a very long day.

Eyes closed, the back of her head resting on a folded towel, Mia mentally counted the number of married Eatons. All of her Uncle Dwight's children were married—Myles, Belinda and Chandra. Married only months apart, Denise and Xavier had made their mother, Paulette, deliriously happy. Two of Uncle Solomon's sons were married. The exception was Levi. Then there was Uncle Raleigh, who was now on his fourth marriage. His daughter, Crystal, who lived with her longtime boyfriend, refused to marry because of her father's inability to remain in a committed relationship.

That left her and Levi. Not only were they the last two unmarried Eatons, but they also had chosen medicine as their career. Dr. Levi Eaton and several other doctors had set up a medical practice in an affluent New York suburb. He'd invited her to New York for a housewarming celebration after he'd purchased a condominium in a luxury building overlooking the Hudson River.

It was Levi and not her father Mia had talked to when her anatomy professor predicted she would never become a doctor. Levi told her that if she did nothing else, she had to prove not only would she become a doctor but also a very good one. She studied longer and harder for his class than the others combined, and when she saw her final grade she called her cousin, screaming that she had done it. She'd earned the highest grade in the class. She knew there would be roadblocks in her life, but Mia hadn't expected someone to dislike her on sight. The experience made her even more determined to accomplish her goal and earn a medical degree.

The water was beginning to cool when she picked up a bath sponge and lathered her body. She stood up and, using the retractable shower attachment, rinsed off the bubbles. It was another fifteen minutes after she'd patted her skin dry, slathered on a scented moisturizer and cleaned the tub before she walked out of the bathroom. The scent of lavender trailed behind her as she entered the bedroom and pulled the nightgown over her head.

Peering through the lacy sheers at the window she encountered a wall of white. The falling snow obliterated everything. She was snowbound, but she realized it could have been worse. She could've been stuck in an airport, sleeping on a chair or curled up on the floor for hours or maybe even days.

For some reason the bath revived her instead of making her feel relaxed. Reaching into her tote, she retrieved her laptop. Turning on the lamp on the bedside table, she sat up in the middle of the bed and waited for it to boot up. She inserted the USB modem and went online. Mia clicked on her mother's email address:

Hi Mom,
Made it to Matewan safely, but will be delayed going on to Jonesburg because of a blizzard. Will hang out with Xavier's in-laws until roads are passable. Call or text me once you return to Dallas. Hug and kiss Dad for me.
Love,
Mia.

She clicked on her New Mail folder, smiling. The man she'd dated off and on while in medical school had emailed her. Dr. Jayden Wright had moved to Denver to work as an acute care physician. He was a third-year resident when she began her internship. A year into their relationship Jayden proposed and Mia turned him down, saying she wasn't mentally and emotionally equipped to juggle marriage and career at that time. They'd parted amicably but continued to see each other whenever they needed a date. Their casual relationship ended once Jayden accepted a position in Colorado.

Hey Mee-Mee,
Hope you're doing well. Thought about you and decided to write. Let me know what you're up to. Love always, Jay

Mia clicked on Reply and gave him an update. After typing several paragraphs she sent the message then logged off. She had to get some sleep before meeting the Yateses and the Chandlers later that day.

Chapter 3

Mia woke to diffuse light coming through the sheers. The house appeared to be as silent as a tomb. Then she remembered Selena telling her the third floor was soundproof. Folding back the many quilts, she swung her legs over the side of the bed, walking barefoot over to the window. Sitting on the cushioned window seat, she wiped away the condensation with her fingers and peered out the window to find it was still snowing.

When she'd gone to college in Philadelphia, it had been the first time she'd experienced a real honest-to-goodness snowstorm. It had snowed nonstop for two days, and when it finally stopped Philly was buried under more than two feet of frozen precipitation. It had been a weekend and Mia had found herself snowed in with her cousins Belinda, Chandra and Denise, who'd come over to her aunt Roberta and uncle Dwight's house to hang out with Chandra. They had talked to Donna Rice—Belinda and Chandra's older sister—and her twin daughters using a webcam.

Mia felt hot tears prick the backs of her eyelids when she thought about Donna. Her cousin had died, along with her husband, Grant Rice, in a horrific head-on collision when a drunk driver swerved across the road and collided with their car. Earlier, after their daughters had been born, Grant and Donna had named Belinda and Grant's brother, Griffin, as legal guardians to Sabrina and Layla. Ironically, Belinda and Griffin eventually married and were now the parents of three children with the birth of their son, Grant Rice II.

Mia chided herself for becoming depressed when she should have been looking forward and not reminiscing about the past. As a doctor, she'd experienced the miracle of life and the finality of death. But she didn't want to become so far removed from the cycle of life that she became indifferent. She was a scientist *and* a realist, but she was also empathetic—sometimes too empathetic to be a good doctor, she thought.

Stretching her body across the window seat, she closed her eyes, willing her mind to go blank. She'd begun meditating, on the advice of her roommate, who'd shared a two-bedroom apartment with her in downtown Houston. Mia found the exercise calming, and it left her feeling balanced. As an only child she'd grown up pampered and protected. But as she matured, what most people would consider protected and indulged she thought of as being smothered. Even when she'd gotten her driver's license, her mother had arranged to have a chauffeur at her disposal. Of course her friends loved sitting in the back of the limo pretending they were out on the town.

What they couldn't understand was that Mia wanted to do things normal girls did: hang out at the mall, have sleepovers, go to the movies, flirt with boys and attend high school football and basketball games. But for Letitia Eaton, her daughter's sleepovers were catered affairs, and Mia's sweet sixteen was comparable to a high society wedding.

The clock on the fireplace mantelpiece chimed the hour, and she opened her eyes. It was nine o'clock, time to get up and face the first day of a new year.

Mia had showered, shampooed her hair, made the bed and put the bedroom in order when she skipped down the staircase to the first floor. Dressed in a pair of tailored black wool gabardine slacks, a cashmere twinset and a pair of leather ballet-type flats, she walked into a large kitchen to find Selena with three women, all of whom were talking at the same time.

"Good morning."

The trio turned to look at her. Recognition dawned on the face of Selena's mother. With the exception of the gray strands in her hair, Selena was a younger version of Geneva Yates. Even without a formal introduction she knew the eldest woman was Kenyon's grandmother. He hadn't inherited her coloring, which looked like aged parchment, but he did have her cool gray eyes. Her silky, silver hair was fashioned in a bun on the nape of her long, elegant neck.

"Good morning," came a chorus of female voices.

Selena approached Mia, pulling her into the kitchen. "I didn't expect you to be up this early."

"Whenever I wake up, I usually get up. It's been a long time since I've had the luxury of sleeping in late."

"Maybe if you had a husband you'd have an excuse for staying in bed," Lily Yates mumbled loudly.

"Grandma Lily!" Selena and Geneva said in unison.

Lily, a tall, slender, raw-boned woman, waved her hand in dismissal. "Don't 'Grandma Lily' me, because you know exactly what I'm talking about." Her eyes narrowed when she stared at Mia. "You're not going to worry much longer about that, because I see you getting married."

Geneva put down the wooden spoon she'd used to mix a batch of cornmeal. "Grandma Lily, please stop. You're scaring Mia."

"No, she's not," Lily countered, "even though she looks like she would blow away in a strong wind. No, Geneva. This young girl don't scare that easily. Do you?"

"No ma'am."

Lily clapped her hands. "See, I told you."

Geneva gave her mother-in-law a disapproving look. "Please don't start with you seeing visions."

"Why is it everyone else believes me when I see things, but you don't, Geneva? The only time you ever listened to me was when I told you not to marry that good-for-nothing triflin' Jimmy Pritchett. Of course he ended up just where I said he would. In prison! But, then you redeemed yourself when you married my son."

"Mama." It wasn't often that Geneva referred to her mother in-law as Mama. But when she did, Lily knew she was upset with her. "Don't forget that we have a houseguest."

Lily shoved her hands into the patch pockets on her bibbed apron. "Must you be reminded that Mia is family, not a houseguest. In fact, she will…" Her words trailed off before she predicted what she'd seen in the vision that had flashed in her mind.

"She will what, Grandma?" Selena asked.

"Never mind," Lily mumbled under her breath. She'd learned over the years there were some things better left unsaid. "Mia, can you cook?"

The question caught Mia off guard. "A little."

"I can see that, because you're skinny as a rail. Sit down and I'll fix you something to eat."

Mia's gaze shifted from Lily to Selena, who nodded, then back to Lily. "Thank you, Miss Lily."

"None of that Miss Lily business. Call me what everyone calls me. Grandma Lily." She said *Grandma* as if it were a grand title, like Your Highness or Mr. President. Lily Masterson-Yates was proud of her grandmother status, and now at seventy-six she was looking forward to the birth of her great-grandchildren.

"Can I perhaps help out with something? I'm not very hungry."

Selena reached for Mia's hand, directing her to a round oak table in the dining nook of the expansive kitchen. "We were all going to sit down and eat breakfast before we start cooking."

"What about Xavier?"

"He's still in bed. So is everyone else. The men probably won't get up until it's time for the football games. Then you'll have to blow them out of the family room to sit down to eat. Dinner will last about three hours—sometimes four, then everyone retreats to the family room to watch a movie or sleep it off."

"How many bedrooms do you have in this house?" Mia asked.

"Six, not counting the one in the attic. Then there's my grandmother's apartment in the converted garage. I'll give you a tour after we finish cooking. By that time everyone should be up."

"I'm not the world's greatest cook, but at least I can help with something."

"How are you with slicing and dicing?"

Mia smiled. "I know how to use a scalpel."

Throwing back her head, Selena laughed loudly. "Should I be afraid of you?"

"Nah! If I was going to go after someone I'd use a gun rather than a knife."

Selena's eyebrows lifted a fraction. "You know how to use a gun?"

"Girl, please. I'm from Texas. I can shoot the cap off a longneck thirty feet away."

"Well, damn!" Selena drawled.

"There will be no talk of shootin' 'round here," Lily called out. "It's enough I have to see my son and grandson carrying guns like they were attached to their bodies."

Mia leaned closer to Selena. "She heard that?"

"My eyes aren't as sharp as they used to be, but there's not a darn thing wrong with my ears," Lily said sharply.

"Would you prefer I carry a slingshot instead, Grandma?"

All gazes were trained on Kenyon as he strolled into the kitchen. Mia hadn't realized she was holding her breath until she felt slightly light-headed. Kenyon was dressed entirely in black: T-shirt, jeans and thick black socks. He wasn't wearing a belt, and the waistband on his jeans rode low on his waist. He also hadn't bothered to shave, and the stubble on his lean jaw enhanced his blatant masculinity. His cropped black hair lay on his scalp without a hint of curl.

Lily glared at her grandson. "You don't need to be sheriff."

Kenyon ignored what had become his grandmother's mantra, approached her and swung her up off the floor as easily as if she were a small child, kissing her cheek. "Good morning and Happy New Year, Grandma." He released, then kissed Geneva. "Good morning, Aunt Gee."

"Don't you dare pick up me," Selena warned as Kenyon

came toward her. She rested her palms over her belly in a protective gesture.

"Don't worry. I'm not going to hurt the baby."

"What baby!?" Geneva gasped.

Selena affected a sheepish expression. "I'm still not sure. I want to wait until the end of the week to make certain."

Geneva's hand shook as she placed it over her mouth. She was expected to become grandmother of twins in another three months, and now the announcement that her daughter could be pregnant had shaken her normally unflappable composure.

"Why wait?"

Selena exhaled an audible sigh. "I don't have a choice. It's not as if I can wade through two feet of snow to buy a pregnancy kit."

"I have a kit."

Turning slowly, Kenyon stared at Mia. He'd thought her single, but now there was the possibility that she might be carrying another man's baby. "Do you also suspect you're pregnant?"

Mia felt a shiver of annoyance and embarrassment flood her body. If she was or wasn't pregnant, it still was none of Kenyon's business. Why, she thought, was he so interested in her personal life? "No. I am *not* pregnant. But I always carry a kit in my medical bag." She felt a modicum of redemption when he managed to look embarrassed at her comeback.

"Sorry about that," he mumbled.

"Apology accepted." Mia winked at Selena. "Do you or don't you want to know?"

Geneva nodded her head like a bobblehead doll. "Say yes."

Selena stared at her grandmother. "Do you want to know, Grandma Lily?"

Lily sat on a stool at the cooking island. "Take the test, Selena."

"You already know, don't you?"

"Stop badgering your grandmother and take the damn test," Geneva spat out.

Selena jumped as if she'd been struck by a sharp object. She'd never known her mother to be so testy. "Oooo-kay," she drawled. She sighed at the same time she blew out a breath. "Let's go, Dr. Eaton. You just got your first patient."

Mia gave Kenyon her best saccharine grin. "Kenyon, I need you to do something for me."

Inky-black eyebrows lifted questioningly. "What is it?"

"I'm going to need you to help me get to my car. My medical bag is stored in a locked compartment under the hatch."

She'd made arrangements for two drivers, one driving her SUV and the other a rental, to leave her car in Matewan. They were instructed to drive north to Charleston, leave the rental at the airport and take a return flight to Houston. If she hadn't had to attend Denise's wedding in Philadelphia she would've made the thousand-mile drive by herself.

Kenyon held out his hand. "Give me your keys and I'll get it."

"It's upstairs."

He motioned with his head. "Let's go, Doc."

Mia felt the heat from Kenyon's gaze on her back as she walked out of the kitchen. Although the staircase was wide enough to walk two abreast, he decided to follow several steps behind and was no doubt staring at her rear end.

"There should be a key fob under the driver's seat. The

set I'm going to give you has a special key that will open the compartment."

Kenyon smiled, staring intently at the way the fabric hugged Mia's hips and concluding she wasn't as skinny as she was slender. There was no way anyone would ever mistake her for a boy because her hips were much too curvy.

"Why didn't you carry your bag onboard?"

"I would have if I'd taken a private jet. A bag filled with scalpels, syringes and narcotics would definitely raise a red flag. What I didn't want to do was spend my New Year's locked up or having my medical supplies confiscated." She peered over her shoulder once they reached the second floor. "Do you ever travel with your firearm?"

"Not as a sheriff. But I did when I was federal flight deck officer."

Mia stopped suddenly and Kenyon bumped into her. She would've fallen if not for his quick reflexes. "I'm sorry. I shouldn't have stopped like that." The apology was breathless, as if she'd run a long, grueling race. It was hard for her to breathe when Kenyon's arms were around her.

Kenyon wanted to tell Mia he wasn't sorry, because it gave him an excuse to hold her, the curves of her body fitting perfectly against his as if they were interlocking puzzle pieces. "Are you all right?"

No, I'm not all right, Mia thought. Her heart was pounding a runaway rhythm, her legs were shaking slightly and her stomach muscles were tightening with each breath. She took indescribable delight in the press of his hard body against hers and the scent of his masculine cologne wafting in her nostrils.

"I'm okay."

Kenyon released his hold when it was the last thing he wanted to do. "Are you certain?"

If she'd been her mother, Tish Eaton would've feigned feeling faint if only to remain in Kenyon's arms a bit longer. Nodding and smiling, Mia said, "Quite certain. I was a little shocked, because I hadn't realized you are a pilot."

"I *was* a pilot," he said, correcting her.

"Just because you're a sheriff that doesn't mean you don't know how to fly."

"I'm a licensed pilot who no longer flies for a living."

"I see."

Reaching for her hand, Kenyon continued up the staircase. "Ask me, Mia."

She gave him a sidelong glance. "Ask you what?"

"Why I gave it up to police a town with less than six hundred people."

"Why did you?"

A beat passed. "I missed my home and my family."

"But didn't you get time off?"

"Not enough. Now I work around the clock for four straight days, then I'm off for three. I can sleep in my own bed, make repairs to my house in my spare time and I can hang out with family and friends on my downtime."

"So, flying to different cities and countries isn't as glamorous as the travel brochures?"

"Not when you're cooped up in a hotel room trying to recover from jet lag or get enough sleep to remain alert. When I felt as if I couldn't sleep in another strange bed or eat another precooked restaurant meal, I decided it was time to get out." Kenyon followed Mia into the bedroom. "It was years before Selena would allow me or her brothers to come up here."

"Did she have a sign on the door that read No Boys Allowed?"

He nodded, smiling. "How did you know?"

"My friends had brothers who used every trick in the book to get into their bedrooms."

"What about your brother?"

Mia eased her hand from Kenyon's loose grip. "I don't have a brother."

"Sister?"

She shook her head. "I'm an only child."

"So you're a spoiled brat." Kenyon had spoken his thoughts aloud.

Mia gave him a withering look. If she had been Medusa he would've turned to stone on the spot. "So, that's where the questions and snide remarks are coming from. It's because you believe I'm a snob."

"Unless you show me differently, then yes."

"Why? What have I said or done to make you say something so asinine?"

"When you came here for Selena's wedding you walked around with your nose in the air. At first I thought you were probably not used to the smell of hay, but when you didn't bother to interact with any of my relatives I knew then you were looking down on us. And, it didn't help that you kept looking at your watch."

Kenyon's assessment of her left Mia speechless. He'd judged her without knowing anything about her. "You are so wrong," she whispered.

"Am I, Mia?"

Heat that began in her chest, washed over her face, bringing with it a light sheen of moisture. She wanted to smack the smirk off Kenyon's face instead of attempting to explain who Mia Eaton was, then decided it wasn't worth the time disclosing why she'd been so distant that night.

She waved her hand. "Forget it. Let me get you the key."

Reaching out, Kenyon's fingers circled her upper arm, pulling her close. "No. I'm not going to forget it. If I'm wrong, then I want to know why."

Tilting her chin, Mia felt the moist warmth of his breath over her lips. Their mouths were close enough where each could swallow the other's breath. Her gaze moved slowly over sharply defined features that made for an arresting face. However, it was his steely gray eyes that pulled her in, holding her captive. He looked like a large black cat with hypnotic, luminous orbs that had the power to penetrate her thoughts and see how much his presence unnerved her. She didn't want to find herself drawn to a man who had a woman in his life. It unknowingly had happened to her once, and Mia wasn't about to make the same mistake twice.

"Selena is waiting for us."

"Stop stalling, Mia."

She jerked her arm away. "Right now I'm not Mia, but Dr. Eaton. If you want to talk, then we can do that later."

Kenyon stared at her from under lowered lids. She was right. They could talk later because it wasn't as if they were going anywhere—at least not until it stopped snowing and the roads were plowed. He nodded, acquiescing.

"We'll talk later. But it will have to be after the football games."

"Okay." Turning away, she retrieved her tote. Searching in the cavernous leather bag, she found the key chain and handed it to Kenyon. "The key is magnetic, so you have to put them in the right grooves for the lock to disengage."

Kenyon extended his hand, and he wasn't disappointed when Mia placed her smooth palm on his. Tightening his grip, he led her out of the bedroom and down the staircase to the front door. He stopped, sat on a low bench and slipped into his boots.

"Where do you think you're going?" he asked Mia when she reached for her boots.

"I'm going out with you."

"No, you're not." Standing, he reached for his jacket on the coatrack. "This will go a lot faster if I go by myself. What good would you be to your patients if you're laid up after a bad fall?"

Her eyes narrowed. "What if you fall?"

Leaning down, Kenyon brushed his mouth over her parted lips. He winked at her shocked expression. "Maybe I'll fall on purpose just to see how good a doctor you are. It will be the first time we'll have a doctor in the family."

Her jaw dropped. "What are you talking about?"

"My cousin married your cousin, and in my book that makes us cousins."

"Where I come from cousins don't kiss cousins."

Kenyon smiled. "And where I come from they do. Besides, that really wasn't a kiss."

Mia didn't want to debate him. "Whatever," she drawled.

She waited on the porch, trying to see beyond the curtain of white as Kenyon made his way gingerly down the steps and around the house to the carport. Leaning over, she noticed that the carport had been constructed to accommodate at least half a dozen vehicles and that snow had accumulated only around the tires. Thankfully her Volvo was the last one parked beside Kenyon's black Yukon. It took all of three minutes for him to retrieve her bag and make it back to the house.

"Nice bag," he said, handing it to her.

"Thank you." Her parents had given her the more feminine version of the medical bag in brown crocodile with her monogram in gold as a gift when she passed the examination to earn her medical degree. A combination lock had replaced the regular key-type lock.

She headed for the kitchen, walking in and finding Selena sitting on a stool while her mother and grandmother were basting a large, fresh ham. Mia motioned to Selena to follow her.

"I'm going to give you a small paper cup. Void in the cup and then leave it on the vanity in the bathroom. I'll take care of the rest."

Selena held up the cup. "It's so small."

"I only need a few drops."

"We'll use the bathroom off the family room."

Mia followed Selena into the family room. She sat down to wait on a leather sectional arranged in front of a large flat-screen television. There were club chairs with matching ottomans, floor and table lamps and a commercial popcorn machine. She glanced around the room, looking for a refrigerator that would be stocked with beer. The space wasn't as much a family room as a man cave. Ashes in the fireplace were evidence of a recent fire.

Selena had mentioned her great-grandfather and grandfather had built the house, and she wondered how many years it had taken them to complete the three-story, multiroom farmhouse. There was no doubt they'd taken meticulous care in selecting the wood for the floors, staircase, banister and newel posts. They weren't carpenters or furniture makers, but artisans.

"It's done."

She turned to find Selena standing only a few feet away. The expectant look on her face spoke volumes. Selena wanted to be pregnant.

"I'll be back with the results in a few minutes," Mia said. She removed a pair of gloves from her bag and a box with a wand. She walked into the bathroom. The space contained a free-standing shower, commode, sink and vanity. Slipping on the gloves, she removed the wand, dipping it into the cup. By the time she'd emptied the remaining liquid into the toilet then rinsed and discarded the cup in a plastic-lined wastebasket, the results of the test were visible.

"Selena," she called. "Come and look."

With wide eyes, the pastry chef walked tentatively into the bathroom. The readout on the wand indicated she was pregnant. "I can't believe it," she chanted over and over. "I just didn't think it would happen so quickly."

Mia smiled as she placed the wand in the box, leaving it and the gloves in the basket. Together, they left the bathroom. "Do you want to know your due date?" With tears streaming down her cheeks, Selena nodded. "I need to know the first date of your last period."

Selena mentally calculated. "November twenty-third."

Mia reached into her bag again, this time taking out a round object that spun like a pinwheel. "November twenty-third," she said under her breath, "would make your due date August thirtieth." She wasn't given time to react when Selena threw her arms around her neck, hugging her tightly. "Congratulations."

"Thank you, thank you, thank you!" Selena took off running, while Mia closed her bag.

"It looks as if you've made someone very, very happy."

Mia looked up to find Kenyon leaning against the carved oak door, powerful arms crossed over his chest. "It was the news she was hoping for."

"What about you, Mia?"

"What about me?" she asked.

"Do you want children?"

An uncomfortable silence followed his query. It was the first time any man had asked whether she wanted children.

Jayden had asked her to marry him even though they'd never talked about whether either of them wanted children.

"I suppose I'd like a couple."

"You suppose?"

"If I met someone and loved him enough to marry him, then of course I'd want to have his children."

"Why do you make marriage sound like it's a gift wrapped up in a neat little bow?"

"Why are you so cynical, Kenyon? Please don't tell me you don't believe in marriage?"

His lids lowered, the gesture hiding his innermost feelings. "I believe in marriage. In fact I tried it once."

"What happened?"

"We weren't as compatible as we thought we were."

"Was she a local girl?"

Kenyon shook his head. Closing the distance between them, Mia patted his shoulder. "That's where you went wrong. Next time you should look for someone who is geographically compatible."

"I'll try and remember that the next time I date a woman," Kenyon said over his shoulder when Mia walked past him, the subtle scent of her perfume trailing in her wake.

He nodded, thinking about her response. Maybe Mia was right. If his ex-wife had been a local woman, beyond a doubt they would've remained married. But he was never one to dwell on the past and what wouldn't or couldn't be. He'd dated a number of women since his divorce, yet none were able to touch that part of him that made him want to commit. When he thought about them he was forced to admit that none were like Dr. Mia Eaton—sexy and totally unforgettable.

Chapter 4

By late morning the entire household was awake and buzzing about the news that there would be another Yates later that year. Selena's announcement that she and Xavier were expecting a baby elicited shouting, backslapping and an abundance of good wishes and congratulations.

After a brunch of scrambled eggs, crisp bacon, sausage links, sliced melon, mini corn muffins and fluffy biscuits slathered with butter or Lily Yates's homemade jams and preserves, the men retreated to the family room to watch the New Year's football games.

Wearing a bibbed apron belonging to Geneva, Mia had remained in the kitchen to help out cutting and dicing ingredients for the many dishes that would grace the dining room table for what would become a traditional New Year's celebration.

It was close to four in the afternoon when everyone sat down at the table in the dining room, but only after Geneva had walked into the family room to turn off the television amid shouts and groans from the men.

Mia had been too exhausted at Selena and Xavier's wedding to join in the levity and eat, drink and dance with the Yates family, but working alongside the women in the kitchen, and engaging in conversation with the menfolk as they came to get something to eat or drink whenever there was a pause in the game, made her feel as if she was truly a part of their family.

Her gaze shifted to Roland Yates, who'd recovered from overindulging the night before, as he sat down at the table opposite Geneva. The tall, handsome sheriff of Matewan was grinning like a Cheshire cat. If Selena was her mother's daughter, then Luke and Keith were their father's sons. Both of them were tall, gangly and had inherited Roland's light-brown complexion and ruggedly handsomely features. Mia was surprised when she was told the brothers had married sisters Christine and Cassandra. The identical twins reminded her of delicate black Barbie dolls. The only difference between the two was that Christine was six months pregnant.

Mia had been instructed to sit next to Kenyon, and when she glanced around the long, rectangular table she realized all of the men were seated next to their spouses: Xavier sat with Selena, Keith with Christine, Morgan with Sylvia and Luke with Cassandra. Lily sat on her son's right, while Geneva sat at the other side.

A hint of gray stubble dotted Roland's recently shaved pate as he gave each one at the table a long, lingering stare. "In all of my fifty-six years I can't remember welcoming a more joyous new year. I know I speak for Geneva when I say we are truly looking forward to becoming grandparents. My baby girl is now a married woman, and she and Xavier are expecting their first child." His gaze shifted to his eldest son. "Keith and Christy, we can't wait to meet our twin grandchildren."

Lily placed a hand on her son's. "Are you certain you're sober?"

A rush of color darkened Roland's face. "Of course I'm sober."

Lily gave him a skeptical look. "I'm only asking because your father, God bless the dead, would start preaching like he was in church when he had too much to drink."

Geneva decided to save her husband further embarrassment when he opened and closed his mouth several times. She extended her hands to Selena on her right and Keith on her left. "Grandma Lily, will you please say the blessing."

Waiting until everyone held hands, Lily bowed her silver head. "Peace be within thy walls, and prosperity within thy palaces. Peace be to this house, and to all that dwell it in. Amen." A chorus of *amens* followed as everyone reached for the napkins at their place setting.

Mia leaned closer to Kenyon, her shoulder pressing against his muscled one. "You're going to have to let go of my hand so I can eat," she whispered, staring at the dark stubble on his jaw.

Staring at her under lowered lids, he smiled. "You have nice hands."

"Thank you."

It was with a great deal of reluctance that Kenyon released Mia's hand. He'd spent the morning and most of the afternoon half-concentrating on the images flickering across the television screen. It had been a tradition for as long as he could remember that the men in the family commandeered the kitchen for a Christmas sit-down supper and the women did the same for the New Year's Day celebration. His father had had to repeat a question twice before he was able to focus enough to answer him.

When asked if he was tired he'd lied and say yes, when the truth was he couldn't stop thinking about the woman who was to become Jonesburg's newest resident. Whether in a pair of jeans, or tailored slacks and sweater—everything about Mia Eaton screamed big-city sophistication.

Once his divorce was finalized, Kenyon had promised himself that he wouldn't get involved with a woman like his ex-wife. As long as he and Samantha were living out of suitcases, sleeping together in hotel rooms or touring the world's capitals their lives were perfect. However, whenever they returned to Jonesburg it was as if she would become a different person—someone he'd recognize but not know. She'd complained that she felt as if her spirit had died whenever she'd returned to his hometown.

Kenyon had tried to compromise in order to save his marriage when he'd agreed to move to Chicago and into a high-rise overlooking Lake Michigan. Then, the tables were reversed because he felt as if he was drowning in a mass of humanity whenever he walked the streets of the Windy City. He'd found it too noisy and congested, and the weather much too unpredictable. Either it was too hot or too cold—unlike Mingo County, where there was a definite change of seasons.

He was never able to get used to the steel-and-glass buildings and the lack of trees, grass, gorges and mountains. West Virginia was one of the most picturesque states in the country. It had been a while since he'd thought about Sam, as he'd called her, and he knew it had something to do with Mia. Both were tall, slender and extremely attractive. It was Sam's winning smile and outgoing personality that struck him the first time they were assigned to the same flight—he as copilot and she as a flight attendant. They'd dated for a year. When he decided it was time to make a firm commitment, he proposed marriage. What neither knew when they'd exchanged vows was that their union wouldn't survive their third anniversary.

"Kenyon, are you certain you're not coming down with something?"

His head popped up and he stared at his mother. "Of course I'm certain. Why would you ask?"

"You're very quiet today."

All eyes were on him when he glanced around the table. He forced a smile he didn't feel. "I'm good." And, he was. Physically he was in the best shape he'd been in his life. But emotionally he wasn't as self-assured as he had been before coming face-to-face with Mia Eaton. He didn't know what it was about her that had him thinking and looking for her when he didn't want to.

"I can check and see if you have a low-grade temperature," Mia said in a quiet voice.

Kenyon smiled again, this time his eyes shimmering in amusement. "The last time I played doctor and patient I was sixteen, and the girl and I ended up butt naked."

Mia's hands tightened into fists under the tablecloth. "I didn't go to medical school to *play* doctor," she retorted between clenched teeth.

Kenyon reached for a bowl of hoppin' John—black-eyed peas and rice—ladling a generous portion onto his plate before he held the bowl for Mia. "I'll hold it while you take what you want." He leaned to his left, his mouth only inches from her ear. "I know you're a real doctor. It's just that I don't *want* or need you to examine me."

"Let's hope you never *need* me."

Mia shifted her attention away from Kenyon, ignoring him while she ate and interacted with the rest of the Yateses since he was someone who had already decided she was a snob.

She sampled every dish, finding each one more delicious than the previous one. The smothered cabbage, turnip and mustard greens, tender, melt-in-the-mouth roast pork, fluffy buttery biscuits, potato salad, sparkling raspberry punch and spiced apple cider had her wishing she'd worn a pair of slacks with an elastic waistband.

Geneva stood up from the table. "Is everyone ready for coffee and dessert?" A chorus of groans and nods followed her question.

Mia knew she had to get up and move around or fall asleep. "I'll help you."

Lily waved her napkin. "Sit down, girl. You're a guest here."

"I thought I was family?" The question was out before Mia could stop herself.

Lily rolled her eyes. "You *are* family, but since this is your first time in our home, you're a guest."

Mia debated whether to sit or follow Geneva out of the dining room and into the kitchen. Kenyon helped her to decide. He stood, taking her hand. "I'll help you." Waiting until they were out of earshot, he dropped Mia's hand. "Don't let my grandmother intimidate you, or she'll run roughshod over you every time she sees you."

"I didn't want to disrespect her," she countered.

Kenyon smiled, attractive lines fanning out around his eyes. "It's not about disrespect. Grandma Lily takes her position as family matriarch as her divine right. If she'd been born into royalty she would've been a tyrant."

Mia stopped several feet from the entrance to the kitchen. "And what are you, Kenyon, if not a tyrant? I haven't set foot in Jonesburg, yet you're treating me as if I'm carrying a deadly plague. I'm committed to completing my residency working with Dr. Lyman, and nothing you can say or do will make me leave. Now leave me the hell alone."

Kenyon stood motionless, watching Mia walk away. A knowing smile became a full on grin. So, he mused, the lady doctor had a backbone. It was apparent she was much spunkier than she appeared. Perhaps she would survive and stay, and not run away like his ex. Turning on his heel, he walked back into the dining room to help clear the table. The women cooked and the men were expected to clean up.

The sounds of snow shoveling and a snowblower could be heard through closed windows as Mia sat on the window seat next to Selena in the attic bedroom. The snow had stopped falling and Xavier, Luke and Keith had assumed the task of clearing away nearly two feet of powdery snow. New Year's had fallen on a Saturday, which gave everyone an extra day to return home before beginning the workweek. Instead of flying back to South Carolina, Xavier had reserved a rental car for the return trip.

"Next year when you get together with your family there will be a number of high chairs at the table. After that it will be the kiddie table," said Mia.

Selena folded her legs in a yoga position. "It's going to take a while before the Yates clan can even attempt to catch up with the Eatons—if ever."

Mia folded her legs in a similar position and rested her elbows on her knees. She'd changed out of the slacks and into a pair of sweatpants and matching sweatshirt with a fading college logo. "You could if Christine and Cassandra have multiple sets of twins."

"Bite your tongue. Christy is freaking out because she's not certain how she's going to care for two babies at the same time. My mother has promised to babysit whenever she needs a break, but I have a feeling my sister-in-law isn't going to want to share her babies with anyone, because it's taken her ten years to get pregnant."

"Ten years for her, and two months for you," Mia said, smiling.

"That's because Christy is an overachiever. She doesn't know when to slow down or relax. Last year she and Keith were talking about adopting, but before they could register with an agency she discovered she was pregnant. Enough talk about babies. What's up with you and Kenyon?"

"What are you talking about?" Mia said.

"Do you like my cousin?" Selena asked.

"Like him how?"

"Would you consider dating him?"

"No."

"No?"

"No, Selena. I came here to treat patients, not to get involved with a man."

"I'm not talking about getting involved, Mia. I'm talking about having some fun during your downtime."

The seconds ticked as Mia stared at the pattern on the wallpaper. "Kenyon doesn't trust me. I don't know why, but he thinks I'm a snob."

Selena gave Mia a direct stare. "Did he say that to you?"

Mia nodded. "Believe or it or not, he did."

"Damn. I've never known him to be so rude."

"Maybe he's *not* feeling well."

"Not feeling well is no excuse for rudeness." Selena bit her lip when she recalled dancing with Kenyon at her wedding reception and he'd referred to Mia as stuck-up, when she'd found her anything but snobbish.

A soft knock on the door captured their attention. "May I come in?"

Mia felt pinpoints of heat prick her cheeks, and she wondered if Kenyon had overheard any portion of their conversation. “Yes, please,” she and Selena said in unison.

As Kenyon entered, Selena unfolded her legs and patted the cushioned seat beside her. “Come and sit.”

Crossing his arms over his chest, Kenyon shook his head. “That’s all right. I just came to say good night. Mia, if the roads are clear in the morning, then we can leave for Jonesburg whenever you’re ready.”

Her eyes took in everything about him in one sweeping glance. He’d exchanged his tee for a V-neck pullover. “I’d like to leave as early as possible.”

“How early is early?”

“What about six?”

A hint of a smile played at the corners of Kenyon’s strong mouth. “Let’s make it eight.”

A shadow of annoyance crossed Mia’s face. She wanted to get an early start because she wasn’t certain what she would be faced with once she saw her new living quarters. Dr. Lyman had mailed the key to the furnished one-bedroom apartment above the space where he’d set up his medical practice. She also wanted to spend time with the physician to review patient charts.

“If you want to sleep in late, then you can. My vehicle is equipped with a navigation system, so I’ll be able to find Jonesburg.”

Kenyon’s face became a mask of stone, his eyes glittering like chipped ice. “It’s not about me sleeping late.”

“What is it about, Kenyon?”

“In case you didn’t know, it only stopped snowing a couple of hours ago. The snow emergency probably won’t be lifted until highway crews begin plowing the major highways, then the less-traveled roadways. Unless your GPS can tell you about all of the back roads, then I suggest you wait for me." He bowed as if they were royalty. "Good night, ladies."

"Is he always this grumpy?" Mia asked Selena, as the sound of Kenyon's footsteps faded when he descended the staircase.

"Not really. But, he's right, Mia," Selena said in defense of her cousin. "West Virginia has some of the most beautiful scenery, but it's also most unforgiving. There are valleys, gullies, caves, mountains and abandoned mines. Some people who've lived here all their lives still don't know all of Mingo County. And my grandmother would have a hissy fit if you left before joining everyone for Sunday breakfast."

Mia patted her belly over the sweatshirt. "I can't imagine eating anything for a couple of days."

Selena sucked her teeth. "Please," she drawled. "After living here for a month you'll eat breakfast, lunch and dinner. The air's different and so is the food. Everything is super fresh."

"I'm not much of a cook, so I suppose I'll have to find a good restaurant."

"There's a wonderful restaurant in Jonesburg called the Kitchen. Run by the same family for more than half a century, they serve the most incredible breakfasts. But if you really want some good eating, then have Sunday dinner at Aunt Sylvia's. Grandma Lily is the first one to admit that her daughter cooks better than she does."

"If she invites me, then I'll be certain to accept."

"You don't have to worry about running into Kenyon, because he'll be on duty. Or if he's off duty, then you'll find him working on his house."

"I'm not concerned about running into Kenyon."

There was something in the way Selena looked at her that said she didn't believe her. But Mia was not going to engage her in a dialogue about the sheriff of Jonesburg. He was there to enforce the law, and she was moving to Jonesburg to treat patients. One had nothing to do with the other.

Selena put her hand over her mouth to stifle a yawn. "I guess I'd better try and get some sleep before we head out tomorrow. Xavier plans to drive south through Kentucky to Tennessee, then head east to South Carolina. It will take longer, but hopefully we'll be able to avoid more snow."

Mia stood up. "Will I see you before I leave?"

"Of course you will." Selena rose to her feet and hugged Mia. "Thanks for everything. If I have a girl her middle name will be Mia, and if it's a boy then it will be Micah."

"You have eight months to come up with names—which means you'll probably change your mind half a dozen times."

"First names, yes. Middle names are a lot easier."

Mia closed the bedroom door after Selena left and then reached for the remote control. Opening the doors to the armoire, she clicked on the television and punched in a channel that featured family movies. It was one she'd seen before, but she decided to watch it again because she knew what to expect. It was the classic romantic story line with a handsome widower raising two children before a young woman comes to town, charming him and his children. It ended with a happily-ever-after.

Her eyelids were drooping as the credits rolled across the screen, and she clicked off the television. Mia managed to undress and put on a pair of cotton pajamas and turn off the bedside lamp in record time. She was asleep within minutes of her head touching the pillow.

Chapter 5

Mia understood what Kenyon had been trying to tell her as she drove slowly behind his Yukon SUV. The roads had been plowed, but there was only one passable lane in either direction. The realization of what he did for a living hit her full force when he'd walked into the kitchen earlier that morning dressed in a gray uniform with a holstered automatic. And not for the first time she wondered whether his decision to give up a career as a pilot to become sheriff of a town with a little more than six hundred residents had been a difficult one.

The drive that should not have taken more than fifteen minutes took an hour. A sigh of relief escaped her parted lips when they finally reached the city limits of Jonesburg. Founded in 1803, it had a population of 647. Its chief industry was mining, and there was also a factory that made Christmas decorations.

The downtown business district was all of two square

blocks with a movie theater, post office, pharmacy, bank, combination dry cleaners and Laundromat, a restaurant, as well as hardware, clothing and liquor stores, a florist, butcher, crafts shop, hair salon and supermarket.

Dr. Lyman's office was next to the bank at the end of the street, and her apartment was one flight above the shops. There was no on-street parking, which made the street a pedestrian mall. However, there was a parking lot for shoppers several hundred feet away. There were two parking spaces behind the medical office, both marked as private parking.

Kenyon maneuvered into one of the private parking spots, while she pulled into the other. Mia cut off the engine, exiting her car. The space behind the shops had been plowed, and mounds of snow had been piled more than six feet high in an area that would have accommodated at least four vehicles.

Slipping into his jacket to offset the biting wind, Kenyon approached Mia. She looked surprisingly young with her short hair and bare face. It took Herculean self-control not to stare at the skinny jeans hugging her hips and legs. The Doc Martens didn't quite fit what he'd thought of as her casual-chic style. Even when everyone wore jeans and tees for dinner, Mia had chosen wool slacks and a cashmere sweater.

He extended his hand. "Give me the keys, and I'll go up and make certain everything is okay."

Mia wanted to argue with him but decided against it. As soon as Kenyon examined her apartment and deemed it safe, she would be rid of him. Glancing up, she noticed there were balconies at the rear of each apartment. There were also partitions between each apartment to ensure a modicum of privacy from neighbors. On the other hand, it would be months before she would be able to sit outside to take in the picturesque views of the mountains in the distance.

Shoving her hands in the pockets of her ski jacket, Mia leaned against the bumper of her car and waited for Kenyon to return. It was Sunday morning and the streets were deserted. Relocating to Jonesburg from Houston had been culture shock. She'd grown up in Dallas, moved to Houston to attend medical school and now she would live in a town with fewer residents than her high-rise complex in Houston.

"Mia."

She turned when she heard what was now a familiar voice. Kenyon's accent wasn't exactly Southern, but it wasn't eastern, either. It seemed to be a blend of the two regions. "Yes?"

"You can go up now."

"Should I bring my bags?"

"No. I'll bring them up."

They exchanged keys, and Mia mounted the staircase leading to the second floor. Kenyon had left the door ajar. She cleaned the snow off her boots on the thick doormat outside and then walked into the entryway, where she was met by the lingering scent of pine. It was apparent Dr. Lyman had paid someone to clean the apartment.

The narrow hallway opened onto a larger space that revealed a living room-dining room area. The sofa and matching love seat and dining table and chairs reminded her of something she'd seen in hotel suites. The sofa and love seat were beige with a faint navy-blue pinstripe. She smiled. The tall, narrow windows were covered with plantation shutters, eliminating the need for curtains or drapes. To the right of the dining area was a utility kitchen with the requisite white appliances—refrigerator, stove, dishwasher and built-in microwave. She opened the refrigerator. It was empty, running and clean.

Mia made her way through the living room to the bathroom. It had a shower, tub, twin sinks and a commode. She exhaled an audible breath. All she needed was a bathtub and a comfortable bed. She left the bathroom and entered a bedroom that was much larger than she'd expected. Rays of sunlight streamed through the partially opened shutters at the quartet of windows. The bedroom windows faced east and that meant she would awake to bright sunlight.

Her eyes shifted to the bed. It was the right size. She'd brought linens for a queen-size bed. Beside the bleached pine bed, there were matching bedside tables each with lamps, a mirrored double dresser and a chest of drawers. A pine rocker with a plump cushion was positioned in a corner. The only things missing were area rugs, a radio and a television. She made a mental note to purchase them.

One thing Mia did notice was how cold the apartment was. She reached out to see if there was any heat coming from the radiator. It was ice-cold. Leaning down, she turned the knob, opening it and listening for the hiss of heat coming through the pipes. She straightened up when she detected someone behind her. Kenyon had come into the bedroom with her luggage, tote and medical bag.

"What's the matter?" he asked.

"I'm waiting for the heat to come up."

Kenyon flipped a wall switch. Light shone through the linen lampshades. "I'll check all the lights and the heat in the other rooms and make certain you have running water."

Mia was still standing with her hand pressed against the radiator when Kenyon returned to the bedroom. "It's still cold."

Inky-black eyebrows lifted. "Is it possible Dr. Lyman neglected to have the heat turned on? I know this apartment has been vacant for at least three to four months."

Mia shook her head. "I don't know."

Reaching for his cell phone, Kenyon punched speed dial. "Eddie, this is Ken," he said when he heard his deputy's voice. "I need you to call Dr. Lyman and ask him whether he had the gas company turn on the heat in the apartment above his office. Dr. Eaton is here and she can't move in if there's no heat. Call me back as soon as you speak to him." He ended the call and turned to stare at Mia. "How long has it been?"

She checked her watch. "It's been at least ten minutes."

"We'll give it another five minutes. It shouldn't take more than fifteen minutes for heat to start cranking. I…" His words trailed off when his cell rang. "What's up, Eddie?"

"Dr. Lyman says he forgot to call the gas company. He says he'll do it first thing in the morning. He also said Dr. Eaton can stay with him and the missus until the heat is on."

"Tell him I'll take care of Dr. Eaton. I hope everything has been quiet."

"It's been real quiet. The only exception was that Jerry Lee got into a fight with his wife. She took the keys to his pickup and wouldn't give them back because he'd had too much to drink. He'd threatened to hit her, but she'd already called us to get him so he could sleep it off in lockup."

"Where is he?"

"Mrs. Lee came to get him about an hour ago, and they were so kissy-face and lovey-dovey that it almost made me sick just looking at them."

Kenyon smiled. "As long as no one ended up in the

hospital or morgue, then it was a good start to the new year. I'll stop by and see you later."

"What's the matter?" Mia asked when Kenyon slipped the phone into a case attached to his belt.

Dark gray eyes met a pair of soft browns. "You're going to have to stay with me until the gas company turns on the heat."

"What!" The single word exploded from her.

"Dr. Lyman forgot to call the gas company. And, because you can't sleep here without heat you'll come home with me."

"I…I don't want to put you out, Kenyon. Isn't there a hotel or motel not far from here I can check into?"

He shook his head. "No. And you won't be putting me out. There's more than enough room in my house. You'll have all the privacy you want."

"But—"

Kenyon held up his hand. "No more. Let's go, princess." Reaching for her luggage, he turned and walked out of the bedroom.

Mia resisted the urge to stomp her foot, which she'd done as a child when she hadn't been able to get her way. Closing the blinds, she turned off the light and picked up the tote and the medical bag. Kenyon was standing on the landing waiting for her. He held out his hand and she threw the keys at him. He caught them in midair.

He glared at her. "Weren't you taught that it's dangerous *and* bad manners to throw things at people?" Mia mumbled a curse under her breath as she brushed past him, stomping down the stairs. Kenyon stared at her back, startled. "Did I just hear what I thought I heard?"

Stopping midway the staircase, Mia turned and glared up at him. "What exactly do you think you heard?"

He dropped his gaze. "Forget it," he said, turning and locking the door.

Mia continued down the stairs, pushed open the outside door and squinted in the bright sunlight. "I need my car keys," she said when Kenyon joined her.

"There's no need for us to take two cars. We'll take mine and leave yours here."

All she thought about was getting away from Kenyon, and because she couldn't stay in her unheated apartment she was forced to spend the night with one of the most arrogant, insufferably gorgeous men she'd ever encountered. She'd thought some of the doctors at the hospital where she'd interned were pompous. But Kenyon certainly gave them some very stiff competition in the egotism department.

She was certain she could deal with his arrogance and smugness, maybe even get used to it. But she was uncertain whether she could stop herself from having sensual thoughts whenever they occupied the same space. Mia had found herself so enthralled with Kenyon Chandler that if he'd asked her to sleep with him she would have without hesitation. There was something about his masculinity that stoked her femininity like a powerful magnet.

He took her bags, placing them behind the front seat of the SUV, and helped her as she settled into the passenger seat. Mia fastened her seat belt and stared out the side window as Kenyon maneuvered out of the parking space. She hoped not being able to move in didn't augur any future problems.

Kenyon left the business district, driving another three blocks to the center of town where a monument, rising more than thirty feet in the air, commemorated those from

Jonesburg who'd sacrificed their lives in various wars dating from the Civil War to the present.

He pointed to his right. "Those buildings are Jonesburg's city hall, courthouse, local library and volunteer fire department. The sheriff's department and jail is housed in the rear of the courthouse."

Mia nodded. "How close is the nearest hospital?"

"It's about fifteen miles from here."

"Does Jonesburg have an ambulance?"

"Yes. We had a fundraiser a couple of years back, and this summer we finally raised enough money to replace the old one. All of our volunteer firemen are certified EMTs.

"Damn," he said under his breath when he saw the flashing red lights and heard the warning bells as a red-and-white barrier descended in front of the railroad crossing. Putting the SUV into park, he slumped in his seat. "We're going to be here for a while."

Mia stared at the slow-moving freight train. "What is it hauling?"

"Coal."

That was the last word they exchanged as Mia began counting freight cars, then gave up after twenty-two. "What happens if there is an emergency and the train is passing?"

"We drive five miles south and take a different route."

She stared at Kenyon's distinctive profile. Despite his darker coloring, his features were more European than African. "Have you thought about having a fundraiser for a small medical center here in Jonesburg?"

Shifting in his seat, Kenyon stared at Mia as if she'd taken leave of her senses, wondering how she could be so intellectually gifted and so very naive at the same time. "Are you aware of the state's median income?"

Mia blinked. "Why?"

Resting his arm over the back of her seat, he leaned closer. "What you have on your earlobes would probably be worth about half the median income."

Mia touched the diamond stud in her right lobe. "These were a gift from my father."

"How nice," he crooned.

Her eyes narrowed. "There's no need for you to be sarcastic, Kenyon."

"And, there's no need for you to be so defensive, Mia. I don't begrudge your daddy giving you an expensive gift. But what you have to understand is that you live in West Virginia now, not Texas or even the Commonwealth of Virginia. The economy in this part of the state is very different from the eastern part. I'm not going to give you a history lesson, but I suggest you either go online or get a book from the library and read up on your new home state."

"I'll do that," she drawled.

"Now, who's being sarcastic?" Kenyon taunted.

Mia turned her head, her mouth inches from his. He'd shaved, his jaw smooth as chocolate pudding. She stared at him through her lashes. "I thought I was a snob."

He smiled. "That, too."

She sobered. "What you'd thought was snobbery was fatigue. I'd worked thirty-six hours without sleep. Then I took something that would keep me awake before I got into my car to drive from Houston to Matewan for Xavier and Selena's wedding. I got to the hotel where my parents were staying six hours before we were scheduled to arrive at the church. That's when I crashed. I managed about three hours of sleep before getting up. I don't know how I managed not to fall on my—"

"I'm sorry, Mia," Kenyon interrupted. "I shouldn't have judged you. Will you forgive me?"

The seconds ticked as they stared, both aware of the intense growing attraction for the other. "It's the new year. And right now I'm feeling very magnanimous, so I'm going to accept your apology."

Smiling, Kenyon shook his head. "You just have to get the digs in, don't you?"

"I don't know what you're talking about."

"What if it wasn't the new year and you weren't feeling magnanimous? Would you have accepted my apology?"

"No," she said without hesitation.

There came a pause. "Do you like men?"

Mia frowned. "What kind of question is that?"

"Just answer the question, Mia. Do you like men?"

"Of course I like them."

"Have any of them done you wrong?"

"No."

"So you don't have a grudge against men?"

"No." Her voice had risen slightly.

"That's good to know."

Mia angled her head. She would have to be completely clueless not to know Kenyon Chandler was interested in her. And she would be in denial if she said she wasn't attracted to him. As a teenager she'd played the usual head games with boys, but once she became an adult she realized how dangerous it could be. She'd learned never to lead a man on and then reject him. And she had also made it a practice not to date anyone she really didn't like.

When Selena had asked whether she would consider dating Kenyon, she'd told her no when she'd wanted to say yes. Selena's cousin was so sexy that when Mia was around Kenyon, she felt she was breathing rarified air that left her feeling slightly light-headed.

"Why is it good to know?" she asked Kenyon

"You don't know?"

Mia shook her head.

"I thought maybe I could take you out whenever our schedules don't conflict."

She smiled. "I'd like that," she said truthfully.

His jaw dropped. "You would?" As soon as the question slipped past his lips Kenyon wanted to retract it. But it was too late.

"Why are you so shocked, Kenyon? Did you really think the *snob* wouldn't go out with you?"

He flashed a sheepish grin. "I'd like you to promise one thing."

"What's that?"

"We never mention the word *snob* again."

Mia held up her hand, extending her little finger. "Pinky swear."

Leaning closer and ignoring her finger, Kenyon's lips brushed against hers. "Kissy swear," he crooned.

She inhaled his body's natural scent mingling with a subtle masculine cologne that had notes of bergamot and sandalwood. Her fingers curled into fists to keep from reaching up and cradling his face.

When her hands did move up it was to gently push him back. He was too close, too potent—everything about him was overwhelming. "Kissy swear," she responded.

The last freight car on the train rumbled past, and the spell was broken. Kenyon turned his attention to the line of cars on the other side of the railroad crossing. Shifting into gear, he drove over the tracks, accelerating as he took a road leading to his home.

"I want you to promise me something, Kenyon," Mia said after a comfortable silence.

"What am I promising?"

"If we decide to stop seeing each other we'll handle it like adults."

"Are you talking about histrionics?"

"Yes."

"I don't have to promise that, Mia. I've never been one to impose my will or force a woman to stay with me. That's not my style." When Sam wanted out of their marriage Kenyon didn't contest it or try to get her to change her mind, and in the end he knew it was best for both of them.

Mia closed her eyes, sighing in relief. "And I promise not to go off on you when you decide you want out."

"That's not going to happen," Kenyon countered. "You're much too intoxicating to take up with then put aside."

"You've come to that conclusion after two days?"

"It's been more than two days."

"But we were only introduced to each other—"

"I know when we were formally introduced. I'm talking about seeing you for the first time at Selena's wedding reception." Kenyon gave her a quick glance, seeing confusion on her face. "I thought you were stunning."

Mia lowered her gaze, unaware of how endearing the gesture was. "Thank you. But don't you think you're taking a risk dating me when you don't do well with women who are geographically undesirable?"

He laughed loudly, throwing back his head. "That's where you're wrong, princess. You now have a Jonesburg address, which makes you geographically very desirable." He drove into the driveway leading to his house. The landscaping company that cut and maintained his grass and garden also did snow removal. "Honey, I'm home," he said in his best Ricky Ricardo imitation.

Mia stared through the windshield at a barn that had been converted into a house. Instead of the ubiquitous red it was painted a battleship gray, with white shutters [illegible] studded with pinecones and with a velvet red bow was attached to the front door. A snow-covered tarp, held in place by wooden planks, was stretched over an addition that was under construction on the north side of the building. She recalled Kenyon saying he wanted to make repairs to his home in his spare time.

She was still staring at the structure when Kenyon came around to open the passenger-side door. "Come on, princess. Let's go inside."

"How old is this barn?" Mia asked, as he lifted her effortlessly off the seat to stand beside him.

"Court records indicate that the house that once stood on this property was built around 1810."

"What happened to the house?"

"I had it demolished, because it would've been too costly to renovate it, even if I'd done it myself. The barn was in much better condition, so I decided to convert it. It's taken me more than four years to make it habitable. It was one of the best decisions I've ever made because a very small investment has given me a house with more than eight thousand square feet of living space."

Now Mia understood why he had calluses on his hands. "What's going into the addition?"

Kenyon unlocked the door, then disarmed the security device. "It's going to be a two-bedroom guesthouse."

"How many rooms do you have in the main house?"

"There are five bedrooms and six and a half baths. I've committed to hosting this year's Christmas and New Year's get-togethers. With Christy expecting twins, and now that Selena's married and also expecting, I realized I needed more room."

Mia walked in next to Kenyon, her mouth agape. The entire first floor was constructed without walls. Wood rafters were installed in the ceiling, dividing the first floor from what had been the loft. Kenyon told her the finish on the walls was made of thin layers of plaster tinged with pigments, and the result was a surface as smooth as wax.

"The walls upstairs are fourteen inches thick, so what goes on in one bedroom can't be heard in the one next to it."

A recessed fireplace was built into a wall made entirely of brick. Quilted wall hangings and a large woven rug in hues of red, brown, tan and black on the wood floor was anchored by a sectional covered in organic fabric. The wide-plank oak floors in the living room gave way to terra-cotta tiles in the formal dining room.

The gourmet kitchen was a chef's dream. Stainless steel appliances, black granite countertops and two work areas with double sinks provided enough space for six to work side by side with relative ease. Commercial-grade ovens and grills, an exhaust system, warming drawers and a table with seating for twelve was conducive for entertaining small or large groups. A decorative wrought-iron gate divided the kitchen from a fully stocked pantry, laundry room and half bath.

"I have to go out for a while."

"How long do you expect to be gone?" Mia asked Kenyon.

"Not too long. I'll set the alarm before I leave if it will make you more comfortable." He wanted to go into his office and complete a report he would then download to the state's Department of Corrections.

Mia smiled. "Please." Not only was the house large, but there was only one other house in the cul-de-sac.

"There's one more thing I'd like to show you before we go upstairs."

Kenyon led Mia through an archway and down a cobblestone path that opened onto an expansive space. "Behold—the man cave."

"Oh, my word!" she gasped, unable to believe the sight unfolding before her. The so-called man cave was enormous. A large flat-screen TV was mounted on a recessed wall above the fireplace. An off-white flokati rug covered most of the floor. Two leather sectionals, love seats, chaises, a recliner with a footstool in a rich oxblood color, beer on tap, a bar that was long enough to accommodate six stools, a jukebox retrofitted with hundreds of CDs, a pool table, a wine cellar and a popcorn machine similar to the ones in movie theaters provided the perfect retreat for entertainment and total relaxation.

"Are women allowed in the man cave?" she teased.

Kenyon winked at her. "Only those who get security clearance."

"Really? You know what?"

"What?"

"I'm going to be like the dog that waits for her master to leave, then jumps up on the bed. The minute you're out the door I'm going to sit on every chair and stool, have a glass of beer on tap, then kick back and watch TV."

Kenyon was hard-pressed not to laugh. It was apparent Mia wasn't as uptight as she seemed, and he knew dating her would be a pleasant surprise. "So, the doctor has a naughty side."

Mia sobered. "I don't know if I'm naughty, but I'm really looking forward to living and working here."

He wanted to tell her that he was glad she was in Jonesburg, but he didn't want to come on too strong. He didn't know why, but he'd thought she wouldn't agree to go out with him. Being on duty four days on and three days off wouldn't give him much time to see her, but Kenyon intended to make the most of it.

"Jonesburg really needs you. After Dr. Lyman retires we won't have a local doctor. In fact, he stopped making house calls a couple of years ago. The only thing I'm going to warn you about is writing prescriptions for painkillers. We have a lot of folks—especially young people—who complain about pain from sports injuries or car accidents. They'll try and get you to write prescriptions before they go to pill mills to get illegal drugs."

Mia was more than familiar with pill mills. There were plenty of them in Houston. It was all about money. Most were sold on the street for profit.

"I don't plan to write a prescription unless a physician sends me documentation of an injury. I'm not willing to jeopardize my license to support an addict."

"I'm going to give you a pager. If there's a medical emergency, we'll contact you. I'm going to make certain someone from my department will always be on the scene in case someone decides to flip out."

Mia didn't tell Kenyon that her medical bag also contained a small licensed automatic handgun. Her mother's brother was a firearms instructor for the Dallas police department, and he'd taught her how to load, clean and handle a gun before her thirteenth birthday. Once she was old enough to obtain a license, he'd taken her to a gun range to practice.

"It's good to know I'll have backup."

"I'll bring your bags in before I leave. We'll take the back staircase."

The staircase, like the one off the living room, was built from salvaged lumber. The room Kenyon selected for Mia was the first one as they stepped off the landing. The door was open, and her smile spoke volumes.

"It's perfect."

It was the perfect space in which to sleep, relax or read.

The bedroom was dominated by a toile-covered duvet and an array of pillows piled high on a queen-size, antique, wrought-iron bed. Framed botanical prints covered the plaster walls. And a hand-knit coverlet hung over a rack, along with several quilts.

A built-in window seat with a tufted cushion and an overstuffed club chair formed a sitting area. A low cherrywood table cradled a stack of books and a vase filled with dried hydrangeas. A decorative screen concealed a dressing area several steps from an en suite bath. She smiled when she spied a garden tub with a Jacuzzi.

"Who decorated your home?"

"My mother. Why?"

"It definitely has a woman's touch."

Kenyon ran a hand over his hair. "I bought this place *after* my divorce. Fixing it up was better than going to therapy."

Mia took a step closer, bringing them only inches apart. "I don't want or need to know about your ex, Kenyon. Whatever happened in your life and my life before today is irrelevant. We've decided we're going to see each other whenever our work schedules permit, and that's that. I'm not expecting a declaration of love, because right now there's no room in my life for love. I have another two years before I complete my residency, so any plans I have beyond that will have to wait."

Kenyon replayed Mia's statement in his head. What she'd proposed fit quite nicely into his game plan, because he'd tired of seeing women just to sleep with them. Initially he'd felt as if he was using them, except that they never asked for more than sex.

"I'll agree to whatever you want. If you get hungry while I'm gone, feel free to cook something. Both the fridge and pantry are stocked."

"I doubt if I'll get hungry before you get back."

"I said that in case I get tied up with something," Kenyon responded.

"I'll still wait."

He angled his head before he narrowed his eyes. "You don't cook, do you?" he asked.

"Not much," Mia admitted. "I can make breakfast, but that's it."

"If that's the case, then I'll try and get back soon." It was no wonder she was so slim, Kenyon thought.

Chapter 6

Kenyon maneuvered into his reserved parking space behind the brick building housing the sheriff's department. Since being elected, he'd put in a request and the city council had approved the construction of a tunnel leading directly from the station to the courthouse for transporting prisoners awaiting arraignment. Residents had complained it was too unsettling for their children to see prisoners in handcuffs or leg irons going from the jail into a side door of the courthouse.

Punching in the code on the heavy steel-reinforced door, he waited for the green all-clear signal, opened the door and closed it behind him, making sure that the buzzer sounded signaling that the lock was reset. He glanced at the two empty cells behind a Plexiglas partition. When the cells were unoccupied, that meant no paperwork.

He punched another code on the pad that led directly into the offices where he and his deputies worked. The smell of freshly brewed coffee wafted to his nose. He'd lost count of how many cups of coffee he drank while on duty. On a night when there were no calls, after he'd made his rounds, he would bed down on one of the three cots in the break room and sleep. Other times he wasn't as fortunate, going out on calls that ranged from vehicular accidents, to the occasional burglary, to domestic disputes.

Hanging his jacket on a coatrack, Kenyon entered the area where Eddie Field sat playing solitaire on the department computer. He didn't begrudge his men for playing video games, watching television or reading, because they needed to keep themselves occupied to pass the time between calls.

"Hey, Eddie."

The redheaded deputy spun around, his green eyes sparkling like polished emeralds. Stocky with a solid physique, Eddie Field was an affable but no-nonsense officer. "Hey, boss. All's quiet."

"That sounds good to me." Kenyon sat down at his desk, shaking his head when he saw the report he had to complete and submit before the tenth of the month. His gaze shifted to his deputy. Eddie had retired from the U.S. Army after putting in thirty years as a MP, and then returned to Jonesburg to take care of his elderly, widowed mother. Months later she suffered a debilitating illness that left her unable to control her muscle functions.

Never married, Eddie complained he had nothing to do, and at fifty-five he didn't want to start a new career. When a position opened up for a deputy sheriff he applied for it, and Kenyon hired him after a background check. Police work was all he knew and was something at which he excelled.

"How was your New Year's?"

"It wasn't as bad as I thought it was going to be. Pamela

came by just before midnight to bring me a plate. Oh man, that woman sure can cook."

Kenyon smiled but didn't comment. He didn't get involved in his employees' private lives, because he didn't want them in his. But he'd always wondered how much experience Eddie had had with the opposite sex. Eddie had to know Pamela Murray liked him. Her grandparents had opened the Kitchen more than fifty years ago, and she'd continued the tradition of serving the most incredibly delicious meals in Jonesburg.

"She is good," he said.

"She asked me out."

"Say what?"

"I said Pamela asked me out."

Resting his elbows on the desk, Kenyon gave Eddie a long stare. He'd had his answer. Eddie hadn't had a lot of experience with the opposite sex. What he couldn't understand was how could a man spend three decades in the military traveling the world and not know women.

"Pamela is a good woman."

"Is that's all you're going to say, Ken? That she's a good woman?"

"What do you expect me to say? She lost her husband in a mining accident more than twenty years ago, and she's never taken up with another man in all that time. So count yourself lucky that she likes you enough to ask you out."

Beads of perspiration popped up on Eddie's forehead. Reaching into the pocket of his uniform pants, he took out a handkerchief and dabbed his face. "I'm fifty-five years old and for the first time in my life I'm freakin' out over a woman."

Kenyon smiled. "It could be she's not just *any* woman, buddy."

"She's not, Ken. She's different—special. Whenever I

come within two feet of her I get tongue-tied, my palms get sweaty and I can't even remember my own name. I…I'd rather face some crazed killer with a fully loaded double-barrel shotgun pointed at my chest than…"

Patting Eddie's thick shoulder, Kenyon winked at him. "Let's face it. You're in love with her."

Eddie's expression brightened, a rush of color suffusing his face. "You think so?"

Kenyon nodded. "I think so, Eddie."

"I don't know what it is about her, Ken. The first time I ran into her again after so many years, I felt as if I'd been hit by a jolt of electricity. What I find so strange is that I never paid her much attention when we were kids. I suppose I was too busy trying to get the hell out of Jonesburg because I didn't want to end up working in the mines like so many kids were back then. I remember my father leaving the house before the sun was up to go ten or twenty feet down in a hole. He'd work for hours in the dark. And then when he'd come back up, it was still dark. It didn't matter what color you were when you went down in the mine, because every man who came up looked the same. That's why I joined the army as soon as I graduated high school."

"Those that didn't want to become miners did what they had to do not to follow in their father's and grandfather's footsteps, while others viewed it as a family tradition, much like workers in the auto industry. My grandmother took an oath that her generation would be the last to go down in a mine, and so far we haven't disappointed her."

Kenyon's father was the principal of the elementary and middle school, while his mother was an expert in textile design and Selena's father was sheriff of Matewan. Her brother Keith taught high school math, and Luke was an actuary. He'd joined the Air Force, obtained a college degree and learned to fly before he was granted an honorable discharge, while Selena had graduated with a fine arts degree from Stanford. She gave up an acting career to become a pastry chef and chocolatier. Her patisserie, Sweet Persuasions, located in Charleston, South Carolina, was featured on the Travel Channel. After the airing, orders for her chocolate-infused pastries and candies had increased appreciably, resulting in her going from retail to an exclusively online business.

"You've done well for yourself, Ken."

"You haven't done too badly either, Eddie."

Leaning back in his chair, Eddie stared at the corkboard with fugitive posters from several surrounding states. "I should have married and had a few kids. I probably would've been a grandfather by now."

"It's not too late."

"I don't think so. I'm too set in my ways *and* selfish to consider settling down with one woman. Don't get me wrong," he added when Kenyon gave him a pointed look, "I'm not a womanizer. If I did decide to go out with Pamela I'd never cheat on her."

"And never cheat in Jonesburg!" they said in unison.

Cheating in Jonesburg was like playing Russian roulette with a fully loaded gun. It was too small and everyone knew one another. Gossip and scandal spread faster than a YouTube sex tape.

Eddie professed not to be a womanizer and neither was Kenyon. What he hadn't done since his divorce was date a woman in Jonesburg. If and when he took Mia out, then she would be the first. A smile softened his mouth when he thought about her hanging out in his house. She was the only woman other than his mother to see the inside of his home.

The telephone rang and Eddie swiveled in his chair to

take the call, leaving Kenyon to concentrate on gathering statistics for the report that would have been completed by Lorie Hatcher if she hadn't been on maternity leave. She was expected to return in another two weeks.

For Kenyon, his workweek would begin Monday morning at eight and end Thursday at midnight. Then there was the weekend and Mia Eaton.

Mia sat on the rug on the floor of the man cave, her back propped up against a footstool, and tapped keys on her laptop. After changing into a pair of drawstring sweats, she'd come downstairs to check out the musical selections in the jukebox. Kenyon had loaded it with CDs from a variety of musical genres spanning decades: R&B, pop, reggae, country, hip-hop, blues, classical and Latin. After selecting her favorites, she then went online to read, answer email and shop for warm nightwear, flannel sheets, towels and other items for the apartment.

She hadn't heard or realized Kenyon had returned until she heard him clear his throat. Her head popped up, her eyes meeting his. Staring up at him made her aware of his towering height and the broadness of his shoulders under the sheepskin-lined leather bomber jacket.

She smiled. "I didn't hear you come in."

Kenyon removed his jacket and gun belt, leaving them on the chair as he folded his long frame down on the rug bedside Mia. Leaning to his left, he placed a kiss on her hair. "How are you?"

She smiled. "Good."

"Are you hungry?"

"Not yet."

"We can have either an early dinner or a light supper. It's your choice."

Mia leaned against Kenyon, the curves of her body

fitting perfectly against the hard contours of his muscled frame. At that moment she felt as if she'd known him for months instead of days. "I'll go along with whatever you want."

A chuckle rumbled in his chest. "Now, that's something that can be interpreted several ways."

Realizing her mistake, Mia grimaced. "Let me rephrase that. I'll—"

"Don't bother, princess. I was just teasing you."

Shifting slightly, Mia met his strangely colored eyes. "Why do you call me that?"

His inky-black eyebrows lifted. "Does it bother you when I call you princess?"

Mia wiggled her toes in a pair of thick white socks. "Not really. It's just that no one has ever called me that."

Draping an arm over her shoulders, Kenyon toyed with the hair touching the top of an ear. "Maybe no one ever thought of you as a princess, princess. When you were a little girl didn't you play prince and princess?"

"No. We played king and queen and I was the queen, and not always the good queen."

"I asked you if you could be naughty and you said no. Which is it, Mia? Naughty or nice?"

Kenyon ran his fingertips over the nape of Mia's neck in a gentle stroking motion that sent shivers of delight throughout her. "My mother is a stickler for propriety," she said. "I grew up with her reminding me that I was an Eaton and a Sanders, and that I shouldn't do anything to sully the family name or disgrace my ancestors. So anytime I got the opportunity to misbehave or act out, I did. Whenever my girlfriends wanted to play dress-up, or when we'd pretend we were characters from some fairy tale, I would always play the villain. I always chose the dark roles in school plays. It gave me the opportunity to get into character and stay in character until the production was over. You have no idea how difficult it was for me to act like an adult when I was still a child."

"Did she approve of you becoming a doctor?" Kenyon whispered softly.

"Approve? She was delirious when I decided to become a doctor instead of a veterinarian."

His hand stilled. "You really wanted to become a vet?"

She nodded. "I grew up with horses, cats, dogs, a bird and two aquariums—one filled with fresh water and the other for saltwater fish."

Kenyon closed his eyes, listening as Mia talked about growing up as an only child in a house set on thirty acres with her parents and a household staff that included a live-in housekeeper, cook, groom and landscaper. Her mother belonged to the Junior League, while she'd joined Jack and Jill. She'd become an accomplished equestrian and marksman.

He opened his eyes, easing back and giving her an incredulous look. "You really know how to use a gun?"

"My uncle taught me. I can shoot the buttons off your vest if you were standing twenty feet away."

"Yeah, right," Kenyon drawled.

Mia glared at him. "Would you believe me if I were a man?"

"Your sex has nothing to do with it, princess. The next time I go to the gun range will you come along with me?" he asked.

Mia held out her hand. "You've got yourself a deal." They shook hands.

His eyes moved slowly over her face as if committing it to memory. "Why did you cut your hair?"

"I needed to save time. If I couldn't get an appointment at the salon, it would take me half an hour to forty-five minutes to blow-dry my hair. Once I set my hours with Dr. Lyman I'll know better how to manage my free time."

Rubbing the short strands between his fingertips, Kenyon stared at Mia's delicate profile. There was something about her—something vulnerable that tugged at him and made him want to take care of her. What made it so ironic was that she didn't need taking care of. She was a doctor with a rewarding and fulfilling career ahead of her. She was an Eaton—a descendant of a prominent African-American family who'd made their mark in medicine, law and education.

He didn't have to have a jeweler's loupe to appraise the size and quality of the diamonds in her ears. One stud was the size of the two-carat engagement ring he'd given Samantha—a stone that had cost him four months' pay. Kenyon wanted to tell Mia she wouldn't endear herself to her patients if she flaunted her bling, but he decided to hold his tongue. He'd warned her about writing scripts for those addicted to painkillers, because it fell within the limits of law enforcement. How she dressed or her choice in jewelry was something she would learn to deal with through trial and error.

Rising to his feet, Kenyon reached down and pulled Mia up with a minimum of effort. "After I shower and change my clothes, I'm going to start dinner." Cradling her face, he brushed a light kiss over her lips. "Would you like to help me?"

"I can set the table."

Kenyon kissed her again. "I'm certain you can do more than set the table." He placed his finger over her mouth when she opened it to debate him. "Shush, princess. I'm going to show you what to do."

Mia nodded. She knew arguing with him would end with two results: a stalemate or a contentious dialogue that would threaten their friendship. "I was doing some online shopping and discovered there is a Wal-Mart not too far from here. I searched out portable electric heaters that look like radiators and they have some in stock. I bought two and plan to pick them up tomorrow morning."

Suddenly Kenyon saw Mia in a whole new light. She may have grown up privileged, but her survival instincts had kicked in, because there was always the possibility it would take more than a day to restore gas service. If there was no gas heat, then it was obvious she wouldn't be able to use the stove. Fortunately the apartment had a microwave.

"We can pick them up later. That Wal-Mart stays open twenty-four/seven."

Wrapping her arms around his waist, Mia rested her head on Kenyon's shoulder. "Thank you."

Cradling the back of her head in one hand, he closed his eyes. Why, he wondered, did holding Mia feel so good? He hadn't misjudged his initial attraction to her when he first saw her at the wedding reception, but he had misjudged her when he'd thought her a snob.

"There isn't anything I wouldn't do to help you."

"And I you, Kenyon," she mumbled softly. "After all, we are family."

Pulling back, he stared at Mia as if she'd suddenly lost her mind. "If we're related it's through marriage, not by blood."

"I didn't mean we share DNA. When I said 'family' I meant it figuratively."

He kissed the end of her nose. "That sounds better." He kissed her again, this time on the forehead. "I need to shower and change. Don't run away."

Mia rolled her eyes. "Where am I going, Kenyon? I don't have a car, you live in the middle of nowhere and not to mention I wouldn't be able to walk a quarter of a mile before getting hopelessly lost."

"I guess you're stuck with me, aren't you?"

"I am for now."

The four words stayed with Kenyon long after he'd stripped off his uniform and stood under the warm water flowing from an oversize showerhead in his en suite bathroom. They continued to haunt him when he changed into a pullover sweater, jeans and a pair of well-worn leather moccasins. He took the rear staircase to the kitchen and removed a package of shrimp and two skirt steaks from the freezer, placing the shrimp in a bowl of cold water to defrost. Then he rejoined Mia, who lay on a chaise with her eyes closed, listening to Sting singing "Fragile."

Kenyon lay on the chaise beside her, pulling her gently into the circle of his embrace. "That's one of my favorite songs."

Smiling and closing her eyes, Mia sighed audibly. She couldn't remember the last time she'd felt so relaxed—as if she had no responsibilities, or a care in the world. The first day she'd walked into the lecture hall at Baylor College of Medicine, her life as she knew it at that time was no longer hers to control. If she wasn't in class she was in the library or at her apartment with her face buried in her books.

She'd forgotten men existed until she started going out with Jayden. The brilliant trauma surgeon reminded her she was a woman who'd refused to recognize her own needs, and despite their busy schedules they'd managed to enjoy their brief interludes.

"I like it, too, but 'They Dance Alone' and 'The Hounds of Winter' are my personal favorites," she admitted.

"I don't know why, but I didn't think you would like Sting."

"There's more than blues and hip-hop," she said, remembering their discussion about musical genres. "An old friend turned me on to him." Mia shifted into a position facing Kenyon.

"Are you talking about an old old friend or an old young friend?"

She angled her head. "He's an old *young* friend who lives in Denver. What about you, Kenyon?"

"What about me?"

"Do I have to worry about some woman coming after me because she thinks I'm taking her man?"

"No, and it won't happen in Jonesburg."

Her eyes narrowed. "What about elsewhere?"

"It's not like that, Mia."

"What isn't like that, Kenyon? Should I worry about a woman getting in my face if she sees me with you?"

"No."

A smile spread across her face. "Good, because I don't like confrontation."

His smile matched hers. "Neither do I, but I'm sad to say it comes with the job."

"Do you like being sheriff?"

He lifted a shoulder. "It's a job."

"It's a job," Mia repeated. "I could say the same thing about being a doctor."

"I don't think so, Mia. You have a career."

"So is law enforcement," she retorted.

"Would you mind if we change the subject?" Kenyon asked. Giving up his career as a pilot was another sacrifice he'd made to save his marriage, but it was all in vain. In the end it had nothing to do with where they lived or how many hours he and Sam spent together. She'd finally admitted she didn't want to be married—and specifically not to him, because she didn't love him.

A beat passed, Mia trying to read Kenyon's closed expression. He hadn't moved, yet she'd felt him withdraw. "I'm sorry for prying."

Resting his palm along her jaw, he smiled. "It's not about prying, princess. I just don't want to talk about it now."

"I thought you were going to teach me to cook."

His smile was dazzling. "Let's go."

Chapter 7

"Tonight we're going to celebrate Texas by making steak and shrimp fajitas."

Leaning against the countertop, Mia watched as Kenyon shelled and deveined the shrimp. "Where did you learn to cook?"

"I'm a country boy at heart, and a true country boy knows how to cook. We start with barbecue, then work our way up."

"Yeah, right," she drawled when he turned his head so she wouldn't see his wide grin.

"You don't believe me?"

"Do I really look that gullible?" Mia asked.

Kenyon's hands stilled. "No. But, you do look sexy."

Mia glanced down at her long-sleeved tee, sweatpants and socks. "You need to have your eyes checked. What I'm wearing is hardly sexy."

"It's not about clothes, Mia. If that were the case, then

women who go around with their breasts and behinds exposed would be thought of as sexy and not slutty. Sexiness comes from within. Either you have it or you don't. You have it, so accept it."

For some reason Mia had never thought of herself as sexy. She was tall and wasn't as curvy as she would've liked to be. Whatever curves she did claim disappeared whenever she neglected to eat because either she'd worked or studied around the clock. Seeing patients at Dr. Lyman's office was certain to be less frantic than treating patients in a large city's municipal hospital. And, the fact that she would live above the office would permit her to take time out to take her meals.

Extending her arms, she bowed from the waist, the graceful gesture reminiscent of a graceful swan before it took flight. "I accept, my handsome prince." Mia peered at Kenyon. He looked very uncomfortable. "Are you blushing, baby?"

Kenyon glared at her. "If I was you wouldn't be able to see it."

Closing the distance between them, Mia cradled his face. "Your cheeks are warm. Did I embarrass you, baby?" she asked.

His hands came up, fingers circling her wrists in a loose grip that would permit her to escape. "Be careful how you use that word."

Her arched eyebrows lifted. "What word?"

Kenyon pulled her close, her breasts touching the solid wall of his chest. "Baby."

"What's wrong with it?" Mia asked, her expression mirroring innocence.

"Whenever a woman calls me 'baby' it usually means we're beyond being friends."

Mia went completely still, her heart beating rapidly

against her ribs. Suddenly it dawned on her that she was playing a game in which she could be in over her head. She hadn't had *that* much experience with men—at least not with men who were like Kenyon Chandler. He may have been a small-town sheriff, but he was also a pilot, licensed to fly a commercial carrier.

She swallowed to relieve the tightness in her throat. "But we're not beyond being friends."

Kenyon released her wrists. "If that's the case, then save the 'baby' until we are."

Something in his mocking tone irked Mia. He was back to being arrogant. "What makes you so certain we'll ever be more than friends?"

"If it were left up to me we would be beyond friendship right now. But I've never been one to take advantage of a woman, so it's going to be up to you to let me know when you want to stop being friends."

Mia managed to repress her anger under the guise of indifference. "In other words, thc ball is in my court?"

"That it is."

The rebellious spirit that always lurked below the surface flared up in Mia like a bonfire. She wanted to throw caution to the wind and strip off her clothes and lie with Kenyon, because it had been too long since she'd felt desire or experienced sexual fulfillment. After Jayden, there hadn't been anyone else. Even if she compared Kenyon to her Jayden, her ex-lover would fall far short of Kenyon's overtly blatant sensuality. Looking at him, inhaling the masculine cologne that was perfect for his natural scent and having him touch her was enough to send her libido into overdrive.

She was twenty-eight, an adult and, as one of her friends would say, "a grown-ass woman." Not only was she grown, but she was much too old to play games. Kenyon was the only man she'd met whom she could sleep with and not experience guilt because she hadn't dated him the obligatory two months.

"I'll let you know."

Don't wait too long, princess, or I'll break my own rule about not pressuring a woman to sleep with me. Kenyon closed his eyes, shaking his head as if to banish his traitorous thoughts. He wanted Mia Eaton the way a man dying of thirst needed water, like a starving man needing food, and like someone locked away in solitary confinement for years needing the sound of a voice other than his own. He opened his eyes, suppressed the passion darkening his gray orbs as they held her gaze. "And I should let you know that I'm a very patient man."

Mia blinked as his gaze bore into her. "How long are you willing to wait?"

"I don't know. It could be a year or two."

Her mouth dropped open, unable to process what Kenyon had just told her. She could not believe he was willing to wait a year or two for them to take their friendship from platonic to intimate. "You're going to remain celibate for two years?"

Kenyon stared, complete surprise freezing his features. Again, he couldn't and didn't understand Mia's naiveté. Or was it that she always took everything he said literally? "Who said anything about remaining celibate, Mia?"

An attractive blush darkened her face. "But…but you said we are friends."

"And that we are." He burst into laughter when her mouth formed a perfect O. This she understood.

"In other words, if I'm not sleeping with you, then you'll sleep with someone else."

Kenyon lifted a broad shoulder. "The pendulum can

swing both ways, princess. If not with me, then it can be some other man for you."

Mia took a quick sharp intake of breath, hoping not to lose her temper. "I don't sleep around, Kenyon."

"Didn't say you did. I'm just saying that—"

"I know exactly what the hell you're saying," she interrupted. "And don't you try and pressure me into sleeping with you."

Putting up his hands in a defensive gesture, Kenyon's expression mirrored innocence. "That's where you are wrong, Mia." Without warning his expression changed, his lips twisting into a cynical sneer. "I've never had a problem getting a woman to sleep with me from the first time I became sexually active. But I do have a hard and fast rule—I don't sleep where I eat."

"In other words, you don't sleep with women in Jonesburg."

His expression relaxed into a smile. "You're quite perceptive. But with you I'm willing to make an exception."

Mia stared at Kenyon, totally confused. He didn't sleep with women in Jonesburg, yet he was willing to break that rule for her. Why? What made her different from the other women? "Why me?" she said.

"Why not you?" he replied. "You're only going to be here for a short time, and if the word gets out that we're sleeping together then you don't have to worry about men coming on to you.

"There was a scandal about twenty years ago when a man caught his wife sleeping with a neighbor," Kenyon continued. "The sordid affair ended with the husband shooting and killing his wife and her lover. It was the first murder in Jonesburg in a decade, and people couldn't stop talking about it. The husband killed each with a shotgun blast to the face. He then put them into his pickup, drove to the town square and dumped their bodies for everyone to see. It happened a couple of months before my sixteenth birthday. My father sat me down and gave me a lecture about infidelity. He said if I was thinking about sleeping with a girl, then make certain she didn't have a boyfriend, or better yet wasn't from Jonesburg. Apparently, everyone learned a lesson from that tragedy."

Mia shook her head. "I can understand the boys not wanting to sleep with girls in Jonesburg, but what about the girls? Without dating local boys it really diminishes their chances of eventually getting married."

"The boys who did date Jonesburg girls ended up marrying them. And the ones who didn't married girls from out of town. I was on the football team, so whenever we traveled for a game I was able to meet girls from rival schools. I had a driver's license and a car, so it made it easier for me to date girls outside of Jonesburg."

"You didn't answer my question about Jonesburg girls."

"Those who couldn't find husbands moved away."

"So one tragic incident changed the dating scene for generations?"

Kenyon gave Mia a sidelong glance. "Yes, since that tragedy involved a gruesome murder."

"What happened to the husband?"

"He was sentenced to a life term in an institution for the criminally insane."

Kenyon reached for a red bell pepper and a large yellow onion and handed them to Mia. "I need you to cut these into thick slices. You can use that knife." He pointed to one of several sharp knives in a butcher block on the countertop.

Mia washed her hands in one of the sinks and dried them on a towel. She picked up the knife, cutting the top off the pepper. Her cooking skills were limited, but her dexterity with a knife was exceptional. Even though she was a family physician, she'd excelled in surgical procedures.

"You're pretty good with that blade," Kenyon remarked when he saw her slicing through the pepper and onion like a master chef.

"It comes from using a scalpel."

"Now that's a nasty little instrument," he said, placing his hands under a dispenser. Lemon-infused liquid soap pooled in his cupped palms. Using his elbow, he turned on the faucet and washed his hands to remove the odor of the shrimp. Mia tossed him the towel.

He gave her a tender smile. "Thanks."

She returned his smile. "You're welcome."

Mia bit into a warm flour tortilla filled with steak and shrimp fajitas, the flavors of soy sauce, crushed serrano chilies, lemon and orange zests, pepper and onion, pineapple juice and sherry exploding on her palate. The spicy guacamole condiment was offset by the cool creaminess of the sour cream.

She stared at her dinner partner seated opposite her in the kitchen dining area. The ceiling pendant light bathed him in a halo of gold. Her eyes moved slowly from the jet-black hair, to his steely-gray eyes, down to the fullness of his firm lower lip that she wanted to taste.

"Is it too spicy for you, princess?"

Mia smiled. In the ten minutes since they'd sat down to eat, they hadn't exchanged a word. She was content to eat while listening to the music coming from the radio.

"Have you forgotten that I'm from Texas?"

"I was under the impression the Eatons were from Philadelphia."

"They are, but there are a few of us who strayed. We're in Florida, Texas, Washington, D.C., and South Carolina."

Kenyon stared at Mia over the rim of a glass of lemon-infused water, wondering whether she would be willing to add West Virginia to the list. "Do you plan to return to Texas after you complete your residency?"

Mia shook her head. "I'm taking a wait-and-see attitude. I love being a doctor, but it all depends on how well I connect with my patients. There is no doubt folks here will see me as an outsider because they're so used to Dr. Lyman. Even though this is the twenty-first century, there are still some men who don't like having a woman doctor examine them."

Kenyon winked at her. "I wouldn't worry about that. We don't know how long it will be before Dr. Lyman hangs up his shingle, but when he does they're going to have to deal with whoever takes over his practice—be it you or another doctor."

She wanted it to be her. Mia didn't want to spend two years treating patients she would come to know, then leave to start all over in another city and with another population. "Tell me about the Yateses and Chandlers. Have they always lived in West Virginia?"

"My dad's people were originally from Virginia, but they came here when West Virginia broke away from the Commonwealth during the Civil War. Because of the region's topography, it wasn't conducive to planting cotton or tobacco, therefore slavery didn't flourish. They got into logging and eventually coal mining.

"My mom's people are a bit more colorful. The Yateses came from Alabama. My great-grandfather was one of the African-American laborers who were brought to Matewan as scabs by mine owners to prevent the coal workers from unionizing. My great-grandmother took in wash to supplement their income, and one of the more affluent men in Matewan took a liking to her. He paid her enough so he would become her only customer. When she rebuffed his advances, reminding him that she was married, his comeback was if she didn't sleep with him then he'd fire her husband. And because they were barely making ends meet on his meager salary, she agreed. After becoming pregnant, and not knowing whose child she carried, she finally told her husband."

Completely engrossed in the tale, Mia leaned forward when Kenyon's face appeared to be carved from stone. "What happened, Kenyon?'

"When she gave birth to a daughter with pale skin, straight black hair and gray eyes it was apparent whose baby it was."

"What did her husband do?"

"He went to the man's house to warn him to stay away from his wife, but when he arrived he was told that the man's neck had been broken when something spooked the horse he'd been riding. My great-grandfather walked away, feeling justice had been served. My great-grandparents went on to have three sons, two of whom died in a mine collapse."

"So the little girl is your Grandma Lily." Kenyon nodded. "Are you the only one to have inherited her eye color?"

"So far."

"Why would you say that?" Mia asked.

"Keith's wife is carrying twins and Selena is also pregnant, so the trait may pop up in another generation. I used to hate it when kids would ask me if I was wearing color contacts. After a while I learned to ignore them."

"Were you ever bullied?"

"I had one kid who tried hustling me for my lunch or

my lunch money. I gave him my lunch because I thought he was hungry. He was one of ten kids. Then, I found out he wasn't just hustling me, but other kids, too. The next time he came to me I was ready. When I told him I wasn't giving up my lunch or my money he swung at me. My father, who'd learned to box when he was in the army, had shown me how to defend myself."

"How old were you?"

Kenyon blew out a breath. "I was either nine or ten. I managed to sidestep him and he hit the wall, breaking his hand. His parents came to school, claiming I had injured their son, but my father, who was teaching in another school district, told them they were raising a bully and that there were other kids at the school who would attest to this. Years later Billy and I became teammates when we joined our high school football team. He was a defensive lineman and I was a running back. Any animosity we may have shared in the past never made it onto the gridiron. We went to the same college, and when he married I was one of the groomsmen."

They continued to talk as they ate, the conversation veering from personal to topics ranging from politics, to the economy, to movies. Mia discovered not only did she and Kenyon have similar taste in music but also in movies. Both liked action flicks, but she favored romantic comedies while he liked movies that spoofed other films. They laughed hysterically until tears rolled down their faces when recalling the satirical comedy *Scary Movie* sequels.

Talking about their childhoods gave Mia a chance to see another side to Kenyon's personality. She never would've thought that he would have a wicked sense of humor. He also had a hidden talent: impersonation. He did an incredible impersonation of Simon Cowell, the former judge on *American Idol,* with a surprisingly good British accent.

She was still laughing when they got up to clear the table and load the dishwasher. Together they made quick work of cleaning the kitchen before retreating to their respective bedrooms to dress before leaving to pick up her electric heaters.

Once at the Wal-Mart Mia selected several nightgowns and a set of flannel pajamas. Although Kenyon's house was warm, she still needed them for her own apartment, and she was uncertain when her online order would be delivered.

"Are you certain you don't need anything else?" Kenyon asked, as they walked across the parking lot to his truck. He hit the remote device, unlocking the doors, and then assisted her in.

"Quite certain. I ordered a ton of things online from some of my favorite stores and shops. I'm going to wait until they're delivered before I purchase anything else." Mia also wanted to wait until her steamer trunk was arrived to take stock of whatever else she needed.

With the exception of the lights in the parking lot and the occasional sweep of headlights from passing cars, the landscape was completely dark. Kenyon had hinted that with its mountains, gorges and forests, West Virginia was one of the most karstic areas in the world. Aside from its coal-mining and logging industries, the state was legendary for its political and labor history.

He loaded the boxes with the radiators and Mia's bags, then came around, slipped in beside her and gave her a small plastic bag. "I bought you something."

Mia opened the bag and took out the DVD. It was *Matewan,* a movie chronicling the coal miners' fight to form a union in 1920. "It looks fascinating, but right now I don't have a DVD player. I ordered one along with a radio and a television while you were at the station house this morning."

Kenyon pressed the ignition button, and the engine roared to life. "You can watch it at my place until your get yours."

He maneuvered out of the parking lot, a slight smile tilting the corners of his mouth. Ordering electronic components meant Mia intended to settle in. Sharing cooking duties and eating together reminded him what he'd missed once his marriage ended. He and Samantha had spent so much time apart that whenever they were home at the same time they'd reacted as if it was Christmas morning when, as kids, they'd wake up early to open their gifts.

But interacting with Mia was different. She made him laugh and she made him think of things beyond his cloistered existence. She was inquisitive, and whenever he spoke she gave him her undivided attention. They hadn't known each other a week, yet it felt as if it had been months. She was that enthralling.

Mia flicked on the light over her seat, reading the back of the DVD case. "How many times have you seen this movie?" she asked, turning off the light.

"More times than I can count," Kenyon replied, concentrating intently on the dark road in front of him. It was a cold, moonless night, and there were very few vehicles on the road. He assumed most people were at home, either recovering from too much holiday libation or readying themselves for a new workweek.

He was scheduled to relieve Eddie Monday at eight, but first he would have to drop Mia off at her apartment. Kenyon also had to program a pager for her to use whenever she went out on a house call. He didn't want her walking into a situation where she would be at risk or placed in harm's way.

"When you watch movies you've seen before, do you narrate?" she asked, after he'd driven at least a mile in silence.

"What do you mean by 'narrate'?"

"Tell what's coming next?"

"Hell no! That's rude."

"Just asking."

Kenyon gave her a quick glance. "Why? Do you?"

Mia stared at his profile. The glow from the dashboard cast three long and short shadows over his face. "No. I asked because I used to hang out with someone who'd talk throughout the film, and it would irk me to no end."

"Have you ever gone to the theater and people yell out 'Look behind you!' or 'Don't go in there!' during a horror movie?"

"Yes," she said. "That's why I always go to the last show on a weeknight with the grown folks. I'm not about to get into it with a bunch of teenagers when I tell them to be quiet."

Signaling, Kenyon drove off the interstate and onto a county road. "Are you tired?"

"No. Why?"

"What do you say we have movie night?"

"Are you serving popcorn?" she asked.

"Yes."

"May I wear my jammies?"

Resting his hand on Mia's knees, Kenyon squeezed it. "You can wear anything you want."

Mia giggled. "You might come to regret that statement."

His hand moved up to her thigh. "Whatever it is it probably won't shock me." Kenyon wanted to tell Mia that since becoming sheriff he'd seen it all. He didn't know what it was, but whenever he went out on a domestic disturbance call either the male or female would be in a state of undress or semidress—something he didn't need to see. Those calls were also the most unpredictable, because he never knew when the couple in tandem would turn on him.

"I doubt that, princess."

"We will see."

Kenyon had his back to her when she walked into the family room in a pair of fluffy yellow Tweety Bird slippers and flannel night gown, and her face covered with a thick moisturizer. She'd showered, shampooed her hair and brushed the short strands until they lay against her scalp.

He was ready for their movie night. Two bowls of popcorn and napkins were set on a side table next to the chaise; he'd started a fire in the fireplace and the television was in DVD mode. A black tank top and a matching pair of lounging pants had replaced his sweater and jeans. Although he'd dimmed the track lighting, Mia could still make out the tattoo on his right shoulder: outstretched wings star and U.S. Air Force inked in blue under the logo. The sight of rippling muscle under firm brown skin as he jabbed at the burning embers with a poker made her mouth go dry from the sensual exhibition of bared flesh.

It's not fair, said the voice in her head. It wasn't fair that one man could be so unequivocally masculine and sexy at the same time. Mia had thought herself immune to the naked human body, but Kenyon Chandler had proven her wrong. She visually feasted on his broad shoulders, tapered waist and how the cotton fabric hugged his firm buttocks when he leaned over to replace the fireplace screen. Without warning he turned and caught her staring.

Kenyon stared, opening and closing his eyes several

times as if to clear his vision. When he'd told Mia she could wear anything she wanted he did not want to believe she would look as if she were going to a sleepover with a group of ten-year-old girls. A yellow flannel nightgown dotted with tiny green and white flowers, Tweety Bird slippers that looked like oversize clown shoes and her face glistening as if she'd been dunked in oil were beyond anything he could've imagined.

Smiling and shaking his head, he closed the distance between them. His eyes moved slowly over her face. "You're right. I do regret saying you could wear whatever you want."

Mia affected a sad look. "You don't like it?"

He ran a finger along her jawbone. "You look as if you fell into a vat of butter."

"I'll blot off some of the moisturizer before I go to bed."

Bending slightly, Kenyon scooped Mia up as if she were a child and carried her over to the leather sectional. "What are you wearing? You smell delicious."

"Lancôme's Trésor Elixir."

He nuzzled her neck. "Hum-mm! You smell good enough to eat." Kenyon placed Mia on the chaise, following her down.

"You're exposing me," she exclaimed, lifting her hips to pull the hem of the gown, which had ridden up her thighs, back down to her knees. She gasped audibly when Kenyon settled her between his outstretched legs.

"Better, princess," he whispered in her ear.

"Almost," Mia said, pressing her back to his chest. "That's it."

Reaching for the remote, Kenyon started the movie. Mia's body went pliant, her head resting on his shoulder. He rested his chin against her head, wrapped an arm around her waist and smiled. Never had holding a woman felt so right, so good.

He forgot about the popcorn as he stared at the large screen with unseeing eyes. There was no need for him to concentrate on a movie he'd seen countless times, so often that he knew much of the dialogue. Kenyon was content to sit silently while holding on to Mia. Her breathing changed, deepening. By the time the final credits rolled across the screen, the fire had burned out, leaving the fragrant smell of smoldering wood.

Mia emitted a soft moan when he attempted to move her. That was when he realized she had fallen asleep in his arms. He managed to extricate himself without waking her, then lifted her gently off the chaise and carried her out of the family room to the back staircase and up to her bedroom.

Mia had left on a bedside lamp and had turned back the blankets. The room was neat, everything in its place. Kenyon placed her on the bed, then removed the fluffy slippers. Just as he pulled the sheet and blankets up and over her body she opened her eyes.

"What time is it?"

He smiled. "Bedtime."

Her eyelids fluttered. "I have to wipe some of this cream off my face or it'll leave a stain on your pillowcase."

"Don't move. I'll get some tissues."

Kenyon had told Mia not to move when she didn't want to move. She'd slept more in the past two days than she had in a very long time. It was as if all the sleepless nights she'd spent studying and the double shifts wherein she was able to stay alert because of adrenaline had finally caught up with her. Coming to West Virginia was like living on a farm: early to bed, early to rise.

Kenyon returned, sitting on the side of the bed as he

blotted the excess oil on her face. His touch was gentle, soothing. "Thank you," she said.

"Is there anything else you need?"

She opened her eyes, staring into his. Mia wanted to say she needed him, but she couldn't bring herself to utter the words. "No, thank you," she said instead.

Leaning over, he kissed her forehead, then the end of her nose and finally her mouth. "Good night, princess."

She smiled. "Good night, sweet prince."

Kenyon sat motionless, unable to move. He sat, watching Mia until she fell asleep. He felt like a voyeur, but it was as if he couldn't get enough of her. She was like the song they'd heard earlier that afternoon—"Fragile."

He didn't know why, but he still doubted whether Dr. Mia Eaton would remain in Jonesburg long enough to complete her residency. And if he were a gambling man he would give her six months and no longer. Reaching over, he turned off the lamp and walked out of the bedroom and took the stairs to the first floor. He had to make certain the fire was out and the house was secure before he went to bed.

Kenyon was comforted by the fact he would be on duty Monday through Thursday, because he needed time away from Mia to clear his head and come to grips with his emotions. If he wasn't careful, then he would find himself in too deep. It had happened with Samantha, and he had no intention of making the same mistake twice.

Chapter 8

Mia stood in her apartment living room, savoring the heat from the radiators as she waited for Kenyon to bring up her luggage. She'd apologized to him over and over about falling asleep before the movie ended until he placed his hand over her mouth to stop her. He was scheduled to go on duty at eight, and she had an appointment to meet with Dr. Millard Lyman at nine, an hour before he was scheduled to see patients.

Her eyes followed him as he walked in carrying her luggage. She'd managed to forget he was a law officer until he put on the dark gray wool pants, matching blouse, star, name tag and gun belt with the regulation equipment. She had taken an oath to save lives, and he'd taken an oath to protect lives. However, her career didn't regulate she carry a firearm, and the gun put him at risk each time he answered a call.

"Are you certain I can't bring you breakfast?" Kenyon

asked, setting down the bag next to the sofa. The radiator generated enough heat to make the space quite comfortable.

Mia smiled. "I'll eat something later." He'd offered to take her to the Kitchen for breakfast, but she'd turned him down because she wanted to unpack and make her apartment appear somewhat lived-in. She didn't want to tell him that she'd eaten more in one weekend since arriving in West Virginia than she usually consumed over a three-day period.

Kenyon studied the woman who unknowingly had impacted his life the first time he spied her at his cousin's wedding. She appeared taller, slimmer, in a pair of black stretch pants, matching turtleneck and imported leather slip-ons. She'd applied a light cover of makeup and had fluffed up her curly hair. Mia had also replaced the diamond studs with a pair of small gold hoops.

"I'll work on getting you that pager today."

Mia took two steps, curved her arms under Kenyon's broad shoulders and pressed her cheek to his smooth jaw. "Thank you for everything."

His arms came up and circled her waist. "I'm going to give you the number to my cell. I want you to call me if you need anything."

"Give me your phone and I'll program my number. I have to call the telephone company to hook up a landline." She didn't want to rely totally on her cell phone, because there were a few occasions when she'd forgotten to charge the instrument. After exchanging numbers, Mia hugged Kenyon again. "You be careful out there."

He gave her a bright smile, attractive lines fanning out around his eyes. "Thank you. Have a good day, Dr. Eaton."

Mia froze. Hearing Kenyon call her Dr. Eaton made the reason why she was in West Virginia all the more real.

She'd come to complete her residency, but to also work as a public-health physician.

"Thank you, Kenyon."

"If you're free this coming weekend I'd like to take you out for dinner and dancing."

Her expression brightened. "You dance?"

"Yes, princess, I can dance."

"Okay." She hugged him again, then watched as he walked out of the apartment, closing the door behind him.

Minutes later, Mia was galvanized into action, removing the plastic covering from the brand-new mattress and pillows. She removed a vacuum-packed bag with a mattress cover, two sets of sheets, a blanket and comforter from her luggage. When she'd received the official letter documenting she would work with Dr. Lyman in Jonesburg for the next two years, she'd been offered free housing and a nominal stipend to cover living expenses. *Nominal* was the operative word, because what she would earn in a month would barely cover the cost of putting gasoline into her SUV. However, she hadn't come to West Virginia to make money, because if money had been her goal then she would've stayed in Houston, or joined her father's Dallas practice as a family physician.

Money had never been an impediment for Mia. Her maternal grandmother had willed her only grandchild property, stocks, bonds and a sizable amount of cash. After meeting with Dr. Lyman the next item on her to-do list was opening an account at the local bank. She made quick work of emptying her bag. Her mother had taught her how to pack by putting everything in space saving-storage bags.

Slacks and jeans were hung on rods in the bedroom closet, and sweaters, shirts, socks and lingerie were neatly stored in dresser drawers. The bathroom was next.

Shampoo, conditioner, bath gel, soap, facial cleanser and moisturizer, and an assortment of lotions filled the medicine chest shelves.

After hanging towels and face cloths on the towel racks, Mia opened a diffuser bottle filled with patchouli, inserting the accompanying reeds. It would take hours before the liquid permeated the reeds and the space, but Mia knew she was home whenever she opened the door and detected the fragrance of the essential oil. There were a few more items she needed to make the apartment feel like home, but they would arrive in the steamer trunk.

She mentally made another notation on her to-do list: shop for groceries. Mia smiled. Going to the supermarket in Houston meant getting into her vehicle and driving miles to a supermarket in a shopping center. Here in Jonesburg she could walk to the market. And if she wanted to shop in bulk, then there was always the Sam's Club off the interstate.

Checking her watch, she realized she still had an hour before meeting with Dr. Lyman. She turned off the heaters, slipped off her loafers and put on the Doc Martens. Although the temperatures was now in the low forties and snow was beginning to melt, there was still enough slush on the streets to make boots a necessity. She pulled on her ski jacket, picked up her keys and set off on foot to the Kitchen.

The distinctive smell of bacon and eggs hit Mia full force as soon as she opened the door to the Kitchen. The restaurant was small, rustic. Wooden rafters, planked flooring and round oaken tables and chairs harkened back to another era. Her eyes swept over the space; every table was occupied.

A woman wearing a pale pink uniform and matching

hairnet, balancing a tray of dirty dishes on her shoulder, swept past. "Sit anywhere, honey."

Mia was still standing in the same spot when a tall, gangly man with snow-white hair who bore a shocking resemblance to Abraham Lincoln beckoned her. All he needed was a beard and he could've been the dead president's clone. He was sitting alone at a table for two.

"Over here, Dr. Eaton."

She smiled. If the man knew who she was, then he was obviously Dr. Millard Lyman. A photograph bearing her image was a requirement when she'd submitted the documents for the position. She approached his table as he rose to his feet. Mia offered her hand. "Dr. Lyman?"

The elderly doctor's gnarled arthritic fingers closed around her smaller hand. "That's me. It's a pleasure to meet you in person." His voice was a strong baritone, seemingly coming from deep in his chest.

Mia took a surreptitious glance and their clasped hands. Now she realized why he'd gone into semiretirement. "The pleasure is mine, Dr. Lyman."

"Please sit down."

Millard Lyman stared at the attractive young woman with whom he would work closely over the next two years. He'd gone over her paperwork, surprisingly shocked when he saw her medical school grades. Mia Eaton had aced most of her courses, and the recommendations from her professors had praised her highly for her coursework and dedication to the practice of medicine.

"I didn't expect to see you until later, but would you mind if we talk over breakfast?"

"Not at all." Mia removed her jacket, hanging it on the back of her chair.

Dr. Lyman affected a soulful expression. "I'm sorry about not informing the gas company to turn on the heat.

I was so busy trying to get the apartment clean and ready for you that it escaped me. I think it was because we had a hotter than normal summer and fall."

Mia gave him a gentle smile. "I bought a couple of portable electric heaters. It's amazing, the amount of heat they generate. Don't worry, I turned them off before I left," she reassured him.

A pair of coal-black eyes stared at her. "Let me know how much they cost and I'll reimburse you."

"That's not necessary," she protested.

"Yes it is, Dr. Eaton. One thing you'll learn working under me is that I don't do well with sass. I say what I say and mean what I say. Do I make myself clear?"

Her body stiffened in shock, and she was momentarily speechless. Mia hadn't expected him to come at her as he had. It was obvious he intended to be a hard taskmaster. This didn't bother her as much as it would have if she were a resident in a large hospital. There she would have more than one doctor watching and barking orders at her.

She sat up straight. "Yes, Dr. Lyman. You've made yourself very, very clear. I will accept reimbursement for the heaters."

They engaged in what had become a stare-down. The elderly doctor's lips twitched, then parted in a smile. "I think we're going to getting along famously."

"We will?"

"Yes. You don't scare easily, do you?"

Mia smiled. It was the same question Kenyon's grandmother had asked her. "No, I don't."

Millard angled his head. "Then, you'll also get along quite well with the folks in Jonesburg. They're plain, God-fearing people who wouldn't know how to put on airs if their lives depended upon it. They work hard, much too hard when compared to other parts of the country.

Our chief industry is still coal mining—a harsh and unforgiving work that is among the most perilous in the world. The men go down in the mine, expecting to come home to their families at the end of their shift, but there are times when it just doesn't happen. I've been treating these families for almost forty years, and not much has changed. I am a third-generation physician, and if given a choice I wouldn't leave Jonesburg for all the gold in Fort Knox." He leaned closer. "I'm going to ask you one question, and I would appreciate an honest answer."

"What is it?"

"When I retire, will you be inclined to take over my practice?"

Mia stared, complete surprise on her face. The shock of his question caused the words to stick in her throat. "You're asking me this before I complete my residency?"

Millard waved away the waitress who'd approached their table. "Please give us a few more minutes, Annie Mae."

She inclined her head as if he were royalty. "No problem, Dr. Lyman."

"Judging from your grades and the recommendations from your supervisors and professors, you will complete your residency under my supervision. That is not the issue."

"Taking over your practice is?"

"Yes."

"Why me? Why not another generation of Dr. Lymans?"

"Unfortunately, my wife and I were never blessed with children, therefore it ends with me. I'd written to several medical schools asking for someone to replace me, and you were the only one who'd submitted an application. What I later discovered was that you'd reached out to the West Virginia Department of Health and Human

Services to work as a public-health doctor. I knew then you were exceptional and completely altruistic. I don't have to tell you that as a doctor in Jonesburg you'll never become wealthy. I've done well because my grandfather had the foresight to accumulate property. I currently hold the deed to every store on this side of the street, and the rents I collect are still much lower than the prevailing rates elsewhere. Vacant shops mean people have to spend money traveling outside Jonesburg to purchase what they need." He traced the design on the plastic tablecloth with a knobby forefinger. "Now back to my question. Yes or no?"

A beat passed as Mia pondered his question. "I would be able to give you an answer if I knew my destiny, and because I don't I can't give you an honest answer right now."

"When do you think you'll be able to give me an answer?"

"Ask me again in six months."

Millard nodded, staring at the serene expression on the young doctor's face. He'd found her a lot prettier in person than the mug shot-type photo she'd taken for her medical license. He was willing to bet quite a few single men would be more than interested in his new partner.

"Fair enough. I'll ask you again in June."

Mia lifted an eyebrow a fraction. She'd mentioned six months only because she resented being pressured. What she didn't understand was why he'd requested an answer now when she had the next two years to make a decision as to her future. Mia knew she had the temperament to live and work in a small town, which was why she'd chosen Jonesburg. If not, then she would've stayed in Houston.

"What are your office hours?" she asked.

"I see patients on Monday from ten to four. The receptionist schedules most immunizations on that day. Tuesday is our late night. We open at one and close at eight. The office is closed on Wednesday. The exception is emergencies. Thursdays and Fridays are both ten to four."

"What about Saturday?"

"I used to open on Saturdays from nine to one, but that was before I decided to cut back my hours. My rheumatoid arthritis has been getting progressively worse, and there are days when I can barely hold a hypodermic."

"What if I cover Saturdays?" Mia continued her questioning.

"Are you certain you want to work Saturdays?"

Mia nodded. "Yes."

Bushy black eyebrows lowered over equally black eyes. "You know you'll be on your own."

"I don't think that will pose a problem. If you trust me to work unsupervised, then I'm willing to see patients on Saturdays."

Reaching across the table, Millard placed his hand over Mia's. "This is not about trust. You're a licensed physician, Mia. And that means you can treat patients with or without me standing over you and watching your every move."

Mia reversed their hands, the contrast between her smooth one and his swollen, misshapen knuckles even more apparent. "Would you be opposed to me making house calls?"

Millard winked at her. "Now you're thinking like an old-fashioned country doctor, Dr. Eaton."

She returned his wink. "I take that as a yes."

He nodded. "It is a yes. The folks around here will really like that. Especially the women with young babies and children. It becomes a real hassle when they have to bundle up the little ones to bring them along. Once we go back to the office you'll see that we don't have a lot of space in the waiting area, and the little kids get real fidgety when they have to wait too long. That's why it's good that you're coming on board, because we'll be able to treat patients in half the time."

"On average, how many patients do you see in a week?"

Millard grunted. "You sure do ask a lot of questions, but that's a good thing. It means you're serious."

"I don't mean any disrespect, but I never would've left Texas if I wasn't serious. I would've completed my residency there and then joined my daddy's medical group."

"I hope you don't join your daddy's medical group. We need you here in Jonesburg more than the folks in Texas need you. No more questions." Raising a hand, he motioned to the waitress pouring coffee at a nearby table. "Whatcha eatin'?"

Mia smiled when he'd lapsed into regional dialect. "Where's the menu?"

"The Kitchen doesn't have a breakfast menu. You tell them what you like and they'll cook it up for you."

She ordered French toast, orange juice and coffee. Dr. Lyman ordered his Monday favorite: grits, redeye gravy and biscuits with peach preserves. He sheepishly admitted to having a slightly elevated cholesterol level and had limited his diet to two eggs a week, otherwise he would've topped his grits with eggs and his biscuits with butter.

There was a steady stream of patrons coming and leaving the restaurant. The waitstaff breezed past tables with orders of steak and eggs, chicken fried steak with white gravy, waffles, pancakes, omelets, home fries, bacon, and ham and sausage links. Dr. Lyman admitted the Kitchen had become a favorite with tourists who crowded into the eating establishment for their Southern fried chicken, red velvet cake and barbecue. Several years ago, the grandson of the original owner built an extension onto the rear of the building, where he'd set up a smoker. Depending upon the direction of the wind, the aroma from the homemade secret sauce drifted for miles.

The topic of conversation segued from food to an overview of the history of Jonesburg. Millard Lyman, who had recently celebrated his seventy-second birthday, kept Mia engrossed with the ongoing conflict between miners and mining companies. Every mine explosion or cave-in reopened a wound that never seemed to heal, despite the mine owner being cited and fined for safety violations.

"Do you remember the coal mine explosion at the Upper Big Branch last April that killed twenty-nine men?"

Mia nodded. "How could I forget? I found myself glued to CNN when they covered the rescue and recovery. I'd prayed they would find some of them alive. Talk about tragic."

The elderly doctor's face seemed to crumble like an accordion. "It was as if time had stood still here in Jonesburg, because most folks were remembering a similar explosion that occurred about ten years ago. High levels of methane and carbon monoxide was the cause. Only a year before the company that operated the mine was fined more than three hundred thousand for serious, unrepentant violations, like lacking ventilation and proper equipment, as well as failing to put a safety plan in place. Explosions are preventable if there is proper ventilation."

A shadow fell over the table, and Mia glanced up to find Kenyon staring down at her. He wore a dark gray Western-style hat, and a small walkie-talkie was attached to his jacket lapel. "Good morning, doctors."

She felt a warm glow flow through her when their eyes met, fused. "Good morning, Sheriff Chandler."

He touched the brim of his hat. "Dr. Eaton."

Millard waved a hand. "Forgive me if I don't stand up, Kenyon. My knees hurt like hell this morning." His gaze shifted from Kenyon to the young woman sharing his table. He wasn't so old that he couldn't see there was something going on between the lawman and his assisting physician. "I take it you two know each other?"

"You could say that," Kenyon drawled.

Mia decided to tell the truth. Once she and Kenyon started going out together there was no way they would be able to hide it. Not in a tiny city with less than seven hundred inhabitants. "My cousin just married his cousin."

Millard's heavy lids lowered as he smiled. "Ain't that a kick?"

"What is it, Doc?" Kenyon asked, folding his arms over his chest.

"You know it's not going to go over too well with the single guys when they find out she's your kin." He gave Mia a long, penetrating stare. "I don't know how well you know *our* sheriff, but Kenyon has earned a reputation as a no-nonsense badass who will lock you up for just spitting on the sidewalk. There was a time when petty crime was so rampant that everyone started locking their doors and vehicles. It stopped when Kenyon asked the mayor and city council to install cameras in the streetlights in the downtown area. A week later they caught some kids who were stealing to support their drug habits."

Kenyon glared at Dr. Lyman, because he was giving Mia too much information. When he'd entered the Kitchen he hadn't expected to see Mia with Dr. Lyman. His first impulse was to pick up Eddie's food and walk out, but he changed his mind. He intended to see her openly, and the more people who knew about them the better.

"I just came over to say Happy New Year, Dr. Lyman."

"Kenyon, I have Eddie's order," Pamela Murray shouted across the noisy restaurant.

Kenyon touched the brim of his hat again. "I'd love to stay and chat, but Eddie's covering for me this morning while I'm in court."

Turning on his heels, he walked over to the counter to pick up the deputy's breakfast. He hadn't been scheduled to appear in court until Wednesday; however, the clerk changed the docket and he had to show up or the defendant would walk. He'd been appointed to replace the former sheriff when he'd quit, citing personal problems, and a year later Kenyon ran unopposed for the position.

It looked as if Mia was getting along with the irascible doctor, whose gruff manner intimidated his patients until they got to know him. There was no doubt she would offer a welcome change to the citizens of Jonesburg.

Kenyon clutched the handles of the shopping bag, from which the most mouthwatering smells wafted, and walked to where he'd parked the truck. He drove the short distance back to the station house, thinking about Mia. He tried not to listen to the silent voice in his head telling him that Dr. Eaton was going to be in Jonesburg only long enough to complete her residency, and then pack up and leave.

He'd left Jonesburg for a while, but then he came back to his hometown, seeing it in a whole new light. Yes, it was small and rural, and its people were poor. The town was located in the Appalachian Mountain range, and that meant the terrain was rugged. But in West Virginia he felt a freedom he hadn't experienced anywhere else in the world. Now, he finally understood the state's motto, "Mountaineers are always free."

Kenyon told Mia he wanted to see her when he should've said that he wanted more—something more permanent, like marriage and a family of his own. He wasn't quite sure why his long-repressed need to settle down was suddenly taking on some urgency.

He hadn't understood why he'd purchased property, demolished the house and renovated a barn with more than eight thousand square feet of living space for one person until after Mia Eaton had crossed his threshold and slept under his roof.

He'd had more than a month to fantasize about the woman whom he'd thought of as a snob, a woman whom he'd wanted to dislike, yet who enthralled him. A woman who occupied his every waking moment so much so that he had to exercise every scintilla of self-control not to strip her naked and make nonstop love to her. Dr. Mia Eaton had gotten under his skin like an itch he couldn't scratch.

It was a good thing he was on duty for ninety-six continuous hours, because it would save him from acting like a lovesick fool. Instead of coming to the Kitchen to pick up his meals, he would call Pamela and have them delivered to the station house to avoid running into Mia. He would wait—wait until the weekend to see her again.

Chapter 9

Mia sat on a stool in one of the two examining rooms, entering notes in the file of a two-year-old boy with a mouthful of cavities who fidgeted uncontrollably in his mother's lap. The child was slightly underweight, undersize, developmentally delayed and had missed vaccinations that should've been administered by the time he was a year and a half. His mother had called to cancel her Monday afternoon appointment because she hadn't been feeling well. Mia had the receptionist call her back and reschedule the appointment for Thursday after she reviewed the toddler's chart.

"I'm going to give your son DTaP."

Kelly Webster tightened her grip on her squirming son. "What's that, Dr. Eaton?"

Mia glanced up at the rawboned woman who had given birth to six children in nine years, the last one was only now three months old. Although she was only twenty-seven, a year younger than Mia, she appeared years older. "It's a vaccination to protect Harry from diphtheria, tetanus and whooping cough. He received his first one at two months, the second at four months and the third at six months. The booster may be given as early as a year, but only if it has been six months since the previous one. Harry has an unusual amount of cavities for a child his age. Are you putting him to bed with a bottle?"

Pale blue eyes brimming with tears focused on Dr. Mia Eaton, who wore a plaid flannel shirt and jeans under a white lab coat. She was a welcome change from the family doctor who'd delivered three of her children before she'd opted to have the remaining three in a hospital. She, like most of Dr. Lyman's patients, was accustomed to his gruff manner and threats about reporting parents to Child Protective Services if he suspected abuse or neglect.

Kelly shook her head. "No. But Harry cries for pop during the day."

Mia's hand stilled as she struggled not to become angry at the child's mother. "You're giving him sodas instead of milk?"

Closing her eyes, Kelly sighed in exasperation. When she opened them, they glistened with unshed tears. "I try not to give it to him, but he won't stop crying. Whenever I don't have milk in the house I give my kids whatever I have."

"You run out of milk?"

"Yes. My husband is out of work because he slipped and broke his leg, so money has been tight."

"The sugar in the soda is rotting your son's teeth. It's also making the boy hyperactive. That's why he can't sit still for long. Because you have Medicaid, I want you to take him to a dentist as soon as possible." Mia flipped through the patient's chart, looking for the page with his parents' financial information. "I see in the file that you receive food stamps."

A nervous smile parted Kelly Webster's lips. "Yes, but it's not enough. I usually run out of milk and bread before the end of the month."

"Are you aware that you're eligible for WIC?" Mia had morphed from doctor into social worker. If she'd been on staff at a hospital she would have referred Kelly to a social worker.

"What's that, Dr. Eaton?"

"WIC is an acronym for Women, Infants and Children's program. It's a federally funded health and nutrition program. You meet the guidelines because of your income, you're a new mother, you have an infant, as well as other children under the age of five. Once you qualify, you'll receive what amounts to a check that will allow you to buy canned fish, cheese, eggs, fruits and vegetables, baby food, bottled and concentrated juice, dry peas, beans or lentils, milk, peanut butter and whole grains, including oatmeal, bread, barley."

Rising, Mia reached for the receiver on the wall phone, punching a button for the medical assistant. "Valerie, please make certain you help Mrs. Webster with the paperwork she needs to qualify for WIC."

"I'll have everything ready for her, Dr. Eaton."

"Thank you, Valerie."

Mia placed the receiver back in its cradle. She turned to smile at the little boy with large blue eyes and curly light brown hair. Aside from his teeth, he was only slightly under the normal range of milestones for a child his age. Unlocking a drawer, Mia removed a hypodermic needle and a bottle containing a dose of DTaP, checking the expiration date. Shaking the bottle, she inserted the needle, filling it, and then pushed the plunger to release a tiny drop of liquid.

"Do you want me to hold him, Dr. Eaton? Harry goes wild whenever Dr. Lyman gives him a shot."

"Put him on the table and hold his waist. I'll do the rest." Placing the syringe on the examining table where the child couldn't see it, Mia leaned down until her face was inches from the toddler as she tore open a packet with an alcohol wipe. "What's your name, big boy?" The blue eyes stared at her suspiciously. "Is it David?" He shook his head. "Maybe it's Michael?" He shook his head again. "I don't think you have a name."

"I'm Harry," he shouted excitedly.

In that moment, Mia took his wrist and held it firmly. She swabbed his upper arm, and quickly inoculated him in seconds. Harry's eyes widen, his little mouth forming a perfect O. Mia ruffled his hair. "It's over, Harry."

Kelly stared in amazement. Her son wasn't crying or flailing his arms and legs. "You're incredible, Dr. Eaton."

Mia disposed of the needle, and then took off her gloves, dropping them in a stainless-steel waste can. "It's a trick I learned from another pediatrician. If the patient knows what is coming, then you have to distract them." Reaching into the pocket of her lab coat, she removed a cellophane-wrapped rubber duck. She took off the wrapper and gave it to Harry. "This is your ducky for when you take a bath." The wide-eyed child took the toy.

"What do you say when someone give you something, Harry?" Kelly prompted.

"Pease," he whispered, squeezing the toy tightly to his chest.

"It's thank—"

"It's okay," Mia said softly, interrupting Kelly. "I prefer *please* to *thank you,*" she whispered. She smiled at the child, her heart turning over in response to the joy in his eyes when he kissed his new toy. "You're welcome, Harry."

There was a light knock on the door, and Dr. Lyman walked into the room. "How are you, Harry?"

"No!" the child screamed, huddling closer to his mother.

Kelly cradled her son. "He's not going to give you a shot, baby."

Millard Lyman turned his attention to Mia. "How did it go?"

"He's good. The only thing is he needs to see a dentist."

"Do you want us to call Dr. Evans to set up an appointment for Harry?" Dr. Lyman asked.

"I'll call you and let you know when I have a free day," Kelly said. "It's going to be a little easier now that the older kids are back in school, and with Al home watching the baby."

"If you don't call me I'm going to call you," Millard threatened. "And if you don't call me back you know what's next."

Kelly narrowed her eyes. "You know I've never abused or neglected my children."

"If your son comes here with a mouth filled with decaying teeth then it is neglect, Mrs. Webster."

Mia could see Harry's mother was becoming agitated as she chewed her lip. The young mother had enough stress in her life, with a husband out of work and taking care of six children. "Dr. Lyman, would you mind if I followed up with Mrs. Webster on Harry's dental appointment?"

"Do whatever you want, Dr. Eaton," he mumbled angrily. "Just make certain that child gets his mouth fixed." He stomped out of the examining room, slamming the door.

Mia wanted to tell Millard Lyman his bedside manner needed an attitude adjustment, but it was apparent his patients were used to it. She gave Kelly a reassuring smile. "You can put Harry's clothes on now. Don't forget to see Valerie before you leave, and I'll be in touch with you early next week about setting up an appointment for your son."

She left the room, walking into the small cubicle that doubled as her office, flopping down on a worn chair that creaked and groaned like the hinges on an unoiled door. Everything in Dr. Millard Lyman's medical practice was outdated—desks, chairs and waiting room furniture. There were no plants, wall prints, magazines, a television or pamphlets—the kind of amenities that were commonplace in most doctors' offices.

Her eyes shifted to the telephone. A blinking light indicated a voice-mail message. Activating the speaker feature, she entered her PIN, listening as the recorded voice guided her through the prompts. Mia sat up straight when she heard the drawling feminine voice:

> Hello Mia. This is Sylvia Chandler. I just rcturned from Matewan earlier this morning and Kenyon told me you'd begun working with Dr. Lyman. I'd like to invite you to Sunday dinner with me, Morgan and Kenyon. Please call and let me know if you will be available.

Mia wrote Sylvia's number on a pad advertising a new anti-inflammatory drug. Although the office had closed on Wednesday, it hadn't been a day of relaxation for her. Her steamer trunk was delivered, along with her online purchases, and it had taken hours to empty the trunk and put away its contents. The apartment now appeared lived-in, with a number of photographs depicting family members, area rugs and a collection of potted plants she'd bought from the local florist. A coffeemaker sat on the kitchen countertop along with several cookbooks and magazines devoted to cooking.

As promised, Kenyon had left a pager that connected to his office with the receptionist. She would've liked to have seen him again, but she had been with a patient. In three days' time she'd vaccinated infants, completed health forms for preteens and high school students, performed Pap tests, recorded blood pressure readings, checked blood sugar levels, treated an ear infection and sprained wrist, and confirmed a pregnancy.

Mia thought about Kelly Webster and her six children. Her last pregnancy had been high risk, resulting in her spending the last trimester on complete bed rest. Her mother and mother-in-law had stepped to help with the children, and when Kelly delivered her baby by C-section she was told it would be her last pregnancy and delivery.

The woman was overwhelmed, and life had thrown her a vicious curve when her husband broke his leg and couldn't work. Mia resented Dr. Lyman threatening his patients with charges of child neglect when it was mostly because they were poor. Kelly needed to be educated about nutrition, not have her children taken away from her.

Tearing a page off the pad, Mia jotted down suggestions she wanted to discuss with Dr. Lyman. The phone on her desk rang and she answered it before the second ring. "This is Dr. Eaton." She listened intently to the recorded message confirming the phone in her apartment would be activated before the end of business the following day. Obtaining a landline eliminated the need to use her cell phone and the internet to communicate with her family and friends.

Her head popped up when she saw a shadow fall over her desk. "Yes, Dr. Lyman."

"Do you have a moment?"

"Yes." Mia followed the tall, stoop-shouldered man into his office. She waited until he sat behind his desk before she closed the door and took a chair facing him. "I suppose you want to discuss Mrs. Webster."

Millard nodded, his gaze fixed on the stubborn set of Mia's jaw. "Are you ready to quit?"

Her eyebrows lifted. "Is that what you want me to do?"

"That's not what I asked you, *Dr. Eaton.*"

Mia slowly shook her head. "No. I'm not even close to quitting."

When she'd walked into the examining room to introduce herself to the first scheduled patient Monday morning, Mia knew this was what she wanted to do for the rest of her life. Conferring with a patient one-on-one without the frenzied activity that was so much a part of a large hospital was like a breath of fresh air. There had been only the sound of their voices, not the PA system blaring codes and paging doctors.

Her softer voice, gentle touch and soothing bedside manner were as different from Dr. Lyman's as day was from night. She made certain to warm her stethoscope before placing it on the skin of her patients. She sang nursery rhymes and silly ditties to the children as she examined them, putting them completely at ease.

Sorry, Dr. Lyman, but she wasn't going anywhere. Not when she was beginning to feel welcome among the people of Jonesburg. Its quaint, laid-back charm was infectious. She'd spent her day off shopping in the local shops, aware that the mom-and-pop stores needed the money more than the large chain stores popping up everywhere. Since she lived in Jonesburg, she planned to spend her money in Jonesburg.

Crossing his arms over his chest, Millard leaned back in the worn, cracked leather chair. "I want you to remember that you're a doctor and not a social worker. You're here to treat *my* patients, not become a facilitator for their other social problems."

Clenching her teeth, Mia counted slowly to three. The words poised on the tip of her tongue were guaranteed to make her lose her serving out her residency in Jonesburg, but she wasn't going to let the elderly doctor treat her like a frightened first-year medical student. She was a licensed medical doctor, something he would never be able to take from her, so they were equals when it came to that fact.

They were Dr. Lyman's patients, but they were also *her* patients. What she wanted to tell the cantankerous physician was that it was *his* practice and *their* patients. If he believed she was going to cut and run, then he would soon discover that as the only female Dr. Eaton she was equitable to the male Dr. Eatons. Her father, Dr. Hyman Eaton, had become a prominent ob-gyn in Dallas; her uncle, Dr. Dwight Eaton, had earned a reputation as a respected Philadelphia family practitioner and there was her cousin Dr. Levi Eaton. Levi and several colleagues had established a medical group in a New York City suburb.

"Have you ever considered that maybe some of their physical problems are linked to either social or psychological stressors?"

"If you're referring to Mrs. Webster, then it is apparent she's ill equipped to raise one child, let alone six. I delivered her, watched her grow up and confirmed her first pregnancy. When she came to me at sixteen asking for birth control, my first impulse was to call her parents because I knew she was thinking of sleeping with that no-good slug who would become her husband, but only after she'd had his third baby. I knew if I didn't give her the birth control she would get it elsewhere or end up pregnant. It didn't matter, because she did get pregnant."

"Did you tell her how to use the contraceptive?"

Millard lowered his eyebrows, glaring at Mia. "Of course I told her." He hadn't bothered to disguise his annoyance at being questioned about something every newly licensed doctor knew to do. "When she came to me suspecting she was pregnant I'd asked her if she was taking the pills, and she admitted that her boyfriend had discovered her pills and flushed them down the toilet."

"But…but why would he do that," Mia stammered, "when most guys don't want to become a baby daddy?"

"Al Webster was afraid Kelly was going to leave him."

"Did she have another boyfriend?"

Millard smiled. "It should've been that easy. Kelly was ranked number one in her graduating class and had been offered full scholarships to several prestigious out-of-state colleges. He knew if she left she would either find someone else or not come back to Jonesburg."

"So the SOB sabotaged her."

"Exactly. If I'd been her daddy I would've contacted the colleges, asking if they would be willing to enroll her the following year and then send her away to have her baby so she wouldn't be under the spell of that parasite. Unfortunately, Kelly moved in with Al's folks and it was all she wrote. She had one baby, then another and then the third before Al finally got a job working in the mine and married her."

Mia leaned forward. "I don't intend to become involved in the personal lives of *our* patients, but I know we can do something that can improve their physical well-being and that of their families."

"Oh, so now they are *our* patients, Dr. Eaton?"

Affecting a smug expression, Mia leaned back in the chair. "Didn't you ask me whether I would take over your practice when you retired?" He nodded. "Well, that's not going to become a possibility if you don't at least hear me out."

Millard lowered his head like a bull ready to charge. "What do you want?"

"I'd like us to offer classes in nutrition."

His eyebrows flickered. "It can't be here, because there's not enough space for more than a dozen people to sit in the waiting room."

"There are a few meeting rooms at the library. If we can't get the library, then maybe a classroom at the high school."

Resting his elbows on the desk, Millard successfully concealed a smile when he ran a hand over his face. "Who would facilitate the classes?"

"Every hospital has a dietitian on staff. We could ask one to come to Jonesburg to chair a series of classes."

"Do you think you could get someone to volunteer their expertise?"

"Did I say anything about a volunteer, Dr. Lyman?"

Millard narrowed his eyes. "I told you before I don't like sass, but you seem intent on sassing me."

"What you call sass I consider being assertive," Mia countered. "I've always fought for what I believe in, even if it means butting heads with those in authority. Kelly Webster's baby's teeth are rotting because she gives him soda pop when she runs out of milk. When I mentioned using powered milk she looked at me as if I'd spoken a language she'd never heard. It's all right for her to buy bottled milk or those in a container, but she should always have powered milk as backup until she gets her next allotment of food stamps. I understand the people in this region don't have a lot of money, but it's up to the mothers to provide meals that are cost-cutting as well as nutritional."

Millard waved a hand. "Stop, stop! You're preaching to the choir. I like what you're trying to do. But please answer one question for me."

Mia felt as if she'd won a small victory, because he'd at least listened to her. What she wanted to win was the war. "What's that?"

"Who is going to pay for these classes?"

"I will. And if it goes well, then I'll go online and research whether there is available federal or state funding for nutrition programs. If there is then I'll write the grant, and depending on the funding we'll hold classes in the spring and fall."

"You're going to underwrite the cost from your own pocket?"

"It's only money, Millard," Mia crooned, using his name for the first time. "Didn't you say I'll never get rich practicing medicine in Jonesburg?"

"So now it's Millard?"

"You can call me Mia if you want, whenever we're not seeing patients."

Throwing back his head, Millard Lyman laughed until he could hardly catch his breath. There was no doubt he'd been sent a firecracker of a doctor. At first he had second thoughts about accepting a female, but then decided he didn't have too many alternatives. The intent of many doctors after securing their licenses was to make as much money as they could in order to pay off six-figure student loans. Apparently that hadn't been the case with Mia Eaton. Her father had a successful practice in Houston, and her mother had come from a family who'd leased their land to a gas company when it was discovered it contained deposits of natural gas. The monies they received from the gas company made the Sanderses one of the wealthiest black families in Texas. No, he mused, money definitely wasn't a problem or an issue for Dr. Mia Eaton.

"I'll allow you to call me Millard under one condition."

It was Mia's turn to laugh. "Don't tell me you're thinking of blackmailing me."

"You can call it blackmail, while I think of it as leverage."

"What is it?"

"I want you to give me your answer in three months instead of six. Why are you looking at me like that?" he asked when Mia cut her eyes at him.

"You're nothing more than a hustler."

Millard smiled, a network of lines fanning out around his eyes and deepening the creases in his thin face. "I had an uncle who was a hustler and a pimp. He was so slick that he could talk his way out of any situation. But he couldn't talk himself out of serving eighteen months on a Georgia chain gang when he was convicted under the Mann Act for transporting a fourteen-year-old girl across state lines to have sex with her. The fact that she told my uncle she was eighteen didn't help his defense."

"What happened to him after he served his sentence?"

"He went into the moonshine business after Prohibition was repealed, selling hooch to the locals. He died, as they say, in a blaze of glory when the still blew up, setting his house on fire."

"I was under the impression stills were built in the woods, not near someone's home."

Millard grunted. "That's what most folks did. My uncle set his up in an attached garage. He always said he was going to go out with a bang, and that he did. What about it, Mia? Three months instead of six?"

Realization dawned for Mia when she rethought Dr. Lyman's insistence that she take over his practice. And if she agreed, would he retire sooner than later? If he did, then it would put completing her residency in jeopardy. She decided to ask the question that had been plaguing her since meeting him for the first time.

"How much pain are you in, Dr. Lyman?"

Millard glanced at a spot over her right shoulder. "So, now we're back to Dr. Lyman."

"Just answer the damn question, Millard."

"A lot of pain," he admitted, ignoring her outburst. "My wife has to help me get dressed and undressed."

"What are you taking?"

"I've tried different anti-inflammatory drugs, but they only give me temporary relief."

She wondered if his bad temper was inherent to his personality, or if it was because he was in chronic pain. If it was the latter, then Mia knew she had to step up and assist anyway she could. "Have you seen a rheumatologist?"

Running his hand through his mane of snow-white hair, Millard smiled. "I had an appointment to see one in Charleston, but I had to put it off until I found someone to cover for me."

"I'm here, so why don't you call and make another appointment. Meanwhile, if you want I can give you an injection to offset some of your discomfort."

Millard's smile grew wider. "I believe you're going to do all right here. You have just enough grit to become one of us."

Mia pointed to the telephone on the corner of the desk. "Stop stalling and make the call. Once you make the appointment I'll give you my answer."

"Now who's hustling who?"

Crossing her arms under her breasts, Mia waited for Millard to call his rheumatologist, who was on staff at a private hospital in the state's capital. She nodded when he told her he had an appointment for the following day. "I'll cover the office for you. And I'll give you my answer in March instead of June."

An audible sigh slipped out as Millard felt as if a weight had been lifted off his chest. He'd been diagnosed with the onset of RA at fifty-five, and the systemic autoimmune disease had become a thief—stealing his mobility while replacing it with redness, swelling, warmth and pain.

"After you give me that shot I'm going to dictate a letter to Valerie that will go out to *our* patients that you are joining the practice. We'll include that you'll make emergency house calls, but our office hours will not change. We don't need to open on Saturday because we have one late night to accommodate those working during the day."

Pressing her palms together, Mia smiled and nodded in agreement. She'd gotten what she wanted, and Dr. Millard Lyman would get what he wanted. If he got the treatment he needed to make his RA tolerable, she would be able to remain in Jonesburg and complete her residency.

Chapter 10

Mia pushed the button on the intercom. "I'm coming down."

"Buzz me in, princess."

She pushed another button, disengaging the lock on the outer door to the rear of the building. She'd called Sylvia Chandler, confirming she would join them on Sunday. As promised, Kenyon had made arrangements for them to go to a restaurant just outside Jonesburg's city limits featuring dinner, dancing and karaoke.

Opening the door, Mia waited for Kenyon to come up the staircase. Four days had elapsed since she saw him at the Kitchen, and she'd spent the time trying to recall everything about him. Seeing him again was an indication her memory wasn't as good as she'd believed. He was taller, his shoulders broader and hips slimmer than she'd remembered.

One day Mia went walking through town and hadn't

realized until she stopped in front of Sylvia Chandler's craft shop that subconsciously she'd hoped to run into Kenyon. She was aware he was on duty Monday through Thursday, but she had hoped she would see him strolling through the downtown area or at the Kitchen. There was something about Kenyon that had connected with her in a way no other man had been able to—and that included Jayden.

It had taken her several months before deciding to sleep with Dr. Jayden Wright. And if she'd really loved him, she would've accepted his proposal of marriage rather than use the excuse that she couldn't juggle marriage and career at that time in her life. Mia wasn't sure how she felt about Kenyon, yet there was something about him that would make it so very easy for her to love.

"Where's your coat?" she asked, lifting her chin. His head came down and his mouth covered hers with an explosive kiss that left her struggling to breathe. He had on a black V-neck sweater, charcoal-gray slacks and low-heeled black boots.

"It's in the truck."

"That's good, because I don't want you getting sick."

Cradling the back of her head, Kenyon pressed a kiss on the bridge of Mia's nose. "I wouldn't mind getting sick if I can have you for my personal doctor." Wrapping an arm around her waist, he pulled her close. The sound of her sultry voice coming through the intercom speaker reminded him of what he'd missed. He'd spent the past week hanging out in the station house reading, watching television and playing computer games after he patrolled downtown and an area of Jonesburg with suspected drug activity.

It was when he retired to the break room and lay on his cot that his mind had played tricks on him. He went to sleep thinking of Mia Eaton, and when he woke it was to an erection that had him believing he was going to come out of his skin. It was all he could do not to resort to his adolescent practice of masturbating. At thirty-six he had no intention of reverting to a sixteen-year-old with little or no control over his sexual urges.

Kenyon wanted Mia not to ease his sexual frustration, but to let her know how much he wanted her—in his bed and in his life. His arm moved up as he cradled her face. She was lovelier than he'd remembered. Soft curls were swept off her forehead and over her ears by a narrow velvet headband covered with tiny peacock feathers. Her shiny curly hair closely resembled the glossy feathers.

"You look so adorable," he said, voicing his thoughts aloud.

Mia glanced down at the black wool off-the-shoulder dress with an empire waist and softly flaring skirt ending at her knees. A pair of black opaque tights and matching ballet-type shoes completed her casual look. "Thank you. The headband makes me feel like Alice in Wonderland."

Kenyon's thumbs traced her cheekbones. "Alice isn't what I would consider sexy. You are. By the way, didn't she skip around with that little apron over her dress?"

"It was a pinafore, baby."

Kenyon went completely still, and for a long moment he forgot to breathe. "I thought we talked about you calling me baby."

"What about it, *b-a-by?*" Mia had drawn out the word into three syllables.

"Let me refresh your memory, princess. Whenever a woman calls me baby it usually means we've gone beyond the friendship stage."

Mia felt as if she were drowning, drowning in an abyss of sensual longing that she hadn't realized existed. "I suppose it'll mean we'll have one of the shortest recorded friendships in Jonesburg history."

Kenyon trailed kisses along her exposed shoulders, lingering at the hollow of her scented throat. He knew his feelings for Mia were intensifying, but that had nothing to do with sanity or reason. If he were reasonable, then he wouldn't be in her living room holding her to his heart. If he were completely sane, he would stay as far away from her as possible.

"We'll never stop being friends, princess."

Drinking in the strength of the hard body pressed to hers, Mia felt a gentle peace wrap around her in a comforting cocoon from which she did not want to escape. Kenyon had ignited a fire, a low flame that refused to go out even when they were apart. His presence was like a controlled substance that had to be monitored, taken in small doses lest she become addicted. Maybe it was good they had careers that hadn't permitted them to spend more time with each other, thus making their coming together even more meaningful.

"Are we going to be friends with benefits?" she asked playfully.

Easing back, Kenyon stared at the woman whom he wanted for more than just sex. That was something he could get from a number of women. He smiled. "Benefits don't even begin to tell the story."

"Do you care to expound on that?"

He pressed a kiss to her scalp. "It's not something that can be put into words. I'll have to show you."

The smoldering flame Mia saw in his hoary orbs startled her. Their conversation was going in a direction where if they didn't leave they wouldn't leave. "I just have to get my coat and bag."

Kenyon glanced around the living room when Mia went

into the bedroom. It had taken her less than a week to settle in and make the apartment look totally lived-in. The photographs, plants and rugs gave it a homey feel. White candles and votives in holders and jars covered every flat surface. He made his way across the living room and dining area and into the efficiency kitchen. A trio of colorful ceramic chickens on a corner shelf added a whimsical touch to the space. She'd broken up the ordinary white appliances with splashes of cobalt-blue-glazed flower pots lining the window ledge.

Taking long strides, Kenyon retraced his steps, walking into the bedroom and stopping short when he spied a small pearl-handled automatic handgun next to Mia's medical bag on the bedside table. She'd turned, closing the door to the walk-in closet, her gaze meeting his.

He gestured toward the table. "What's up with the gun?"

"It's licensed," Mia said, slipping her arms into the sleeves of a black wool three-quarter swing coat. She'd taken the automatic out of the bag to clean it and had been in the process of putting it back when the intercom buzzed.

"Do you always carry it with you?"

"I will," Mia confirmed, "only when I make an emergency house call. It's a known fact that doctors carry painkillers in their bags, so I'm not going to risk getting hurt when someone decides to rob me."

Kenyon angled his head as he slipped his hands into the pockets of his slacks. He didn't like it. Mia carrying a gun was like placing a bull's-eye target on her back if someone suspected she had it. "I told you we would cover you on house calls."

"You told me you or your deputy would be on hand if you called for emergency medical assistance. Don't forget you have the EMTs assigned to the fire department. They'll probably get to the scene before me."

"I still don't feel comfortable knowing you're carrying a gun. What if the perp decides to use it on you?"

"What if I shoot the perp, then turn around and treat him for a gunshot wound? And, of course, I'm mandated by law to report it to the police."

"That's not funny," he said, deadpan.

"I didn't say it to be funny, Kenyon." Mia closed the distance between them, patting his shoulder in a comforting gesture. "Unless you mention it, no one will ever know I'm carrying a gun. Fortunately, I've never had to use it." She picked up the twenty-two, placed it in the medical bag and walked back to the closet, where she placed the bag into a safe with an LCD electronic lock. "If someone decides to break in, then they're going to have to try and make it down the staircase with a safe weighing one hundred thirty-five pounds."

"Who put the safe in the closet?"

Mia buttoned her coat, then picked up a small leather purse with a shoulder strap. She put in on, the strap resting across her body. "I asked the men who delivered my trunk to put it in the closet for me."

Staring at Mia through lowered lids, Kenyon thought of her as a chameleon. She'd gone from the ultimate sophisticate at Selena's wedding to casual chic and delightfully quirky with her flannel nightgown and Tweety Bird slippers. The woman standing only inches from him had transformed herself again—this time into an ingenue with the headband, ballet flats and understated dress that showed off her incredibly sexy shoulders and neck. The hem of the dress ended at her knees, displaying her long legs to their best advantage.

His mother, who'd arrived in Matewan several days

before his father, had returned to Jonesburg midweek. Sylvia Chandler had called him inquiring about Mia. She wanted to know if he was helping her adjust to Jonesburg, and when he answered in the affirmative she'd suggested inviting her to Sunday dinner. Kenyon wanted to tell his mother that he'd made plans for he and Mia to spend the weekend together, but held his tongue. After all, he and Mia had the next two years in which to share weekends.

"Are we going out, or are we going to stay here?"

Her soft query shattered Kenyon's musings. Reaching for her hand, he cradled it in his protective grip. "Let's go, princess."

Mia had been to clubs in Dallas, Philadelphia and Houston with their high-tech lighting, state-of-the art sound systems, futuristic bars and décor that made her feel as if she'd gone to another universe. However, nothing prepared her for thc sight that unfolded when she walked into the Tunnel. She felt as if she had entered a subtly lit, overheated coal mine. Now she knew why Kenyon had suggested she leave her coat in the car.

The source of heat came from at least a dozen fireplaces and the couples on the dance floor writhing to the rhythms of a popular classic dance tune that dominated the Top 40 for three months several years ago.

A tall, bearded man gave Kenyon a wide grin before wrapping massive arms around his body in a bear hug and lifting him off his feet. "What the hell is going on tonight? There's so much five-oh in the house tonight that it feels like a law enforcement convention."

Kenyon pounded Billy Lord's back with his fist. "How are you?" he asked when his former schoolmate set him on his feet.

"Good, man. Business is good, the missus is good and the kids are bad as hell, especially my boy."

"Is he shaking down kids for their lunch money?"

Billy turned a bright red that closely matched his fiery red-orange facial hair. "What do they say about payback?"

"What goes around comes around," Kenyon intoned, smiling. Looping an arm around Mia's waist, he molded her against his length. "I'd like you to meet Mia Eaton. Mia, this is Billy Lord."

Extending her hand, Mia smiled up at the mountain of a man who'd lifted Kenyon off his feet as if he were a child instead of a man standing at least six-three and weighing more than two hundred and fifty pounds. And judging from their conversation, she concluded he had been the boy who had bullied Kenyon for his lunch money. "It's nice meeting you, Billy."

Cradling the smaller hand gently within his hamlike grip, Billy dropped a kiss on the back of her hand. "Welcome to the Tunnel, Dr. Eaton."

Her jaw dropped, and Billy tightened his hold on her hand when she attempted to extricate it. "You know who I am?"

Throwing back his head, Billy let out a booming laugh. "I may not live in Jonesburg, but I know everything that goes on there. My mother told me that a Dr. Eaton is now working with Dr. Lyman. You're a welcome change from that old sourpuss. Don't get me wrong, Dr. Lyman is a very good doctor, but I don't remember ever seeing him smile."

"He smiles for me," Mia said in defense of her colleague.

Billy's brown eyes moved up and down her body. "I can see why."

Kenyon knew it was time to put an end to Billy's not so subtle flirtation with *his woman.* The two words echoed in his head, rocking him to the core. He hadn't made love to Mia, yet he'd thought of her as his woman. What shocked him was that he'd never thought of himself as possessive or jealous. But at that moment the emotions made him feel strange and very uneasy. It was all he could do not to reach over and pull Mia's hand away.

"Did you save me a table?" he said instead.

Billy nodded. "Sure did. Follow me," he said, releasing Mia's hand.

The Tunnel was nearing capacity. It was a Friday night, and couples and singles had crowded into the large barnlike building off the interstate to eat, drink, dance and unwind from work and relax after the stress of a holiday season that began a day after Thanksgiving. And, unlike some of the more upscale clubs, the Tunnel had no cover charge, served good food, offered reasonably priced drinks and featured live and prerecorded music on Fridays.

Mia and Kenyon were shown to a table for two, where they were able to observe the raised stage, dance floor and people sitting and standing around a rectangular bar. Removing the Reserved sign and waiting until Kenyon seated Mia, Billy said, "I'll have someone bring you a menu. Enjoy."

"Thanks," Kenyon and Mia said in unison.

She smiled at her dining partner. "This is very nice."

Resting his arms on the table, Kenyon stared at Mia; the light from a flickering candle flattered the gold undertones in her flawless face and made her eyes appeared usually large, dark and mysterious. "Don't you find it a little rustic for your more refined tastes?"

A frown appeared between her eyes. "Why are you going to ruin what I hope will be a wonderful evening by being facetious, Kenyon?"

His expressive eyebrows lifted. "I was merely asking a question."

"And I'm not going to dignify that question with an answer. I take it Billy is the one who bullied you when you were kids?" Mia had deftly changed the topic.

Kenyon smiled, nodding. "Yes. But, as they say, that's water under the bridge. Would you like something to drink?" It was his turn to change the subject.

"I'll have a glass of white wine."

"Are you sure you don't want anything stronger?"

Mia flashed a sexy moue. "No. Wine is good just in case I have to become the designated driver."

Sitting up straight, Kenyon gave her a long, penetrating look. "I've never flown or driven while under the influence."

Reaching across the table, Mia placed her hand atop his fisted one. "I didn't say you did, but if you want to have more than a couple of drinks I wouldn't mind driving back home."

His expression softened. "Do you think you could get back without getting lost?" He'd taken the back roads instead of the county road to avoid the tractor trailers hauling goods cross-country.

"Yes."

Shifting slightly, Kenyon reached into the pocket of his slacks, handing over the key to his truck. "Tonight you're the designated driver." Pushing back his chair, he stood. "I'll bring you your wine."

Mia watched as Kenyon made his way to the bar, raising his hand and signaling one of the four bartenders mixing and pouring drinks for those waiting patiently to be served. Her lips parted in a smile when he reached over a shorter man, handing the bartender a bill. Less than five minutes later he returned to the table carrying a wineglass and a highball filled with ice and dark-colored liquid.

"Shame on you, Kenyon," she crooned softly. "You jumped the line."

"No, I didn't," he said, placing the drinks on the wood table hewn from a tree trunk. "The bartender is Billy's cousin and partner in this place, and we go way back."

Mia picked up her glass, touching it to Kenyon's. "There's a traditional Russian saying I like. 'I raise my glass to wish you your heart's desire.'"

Kenyon's eyes darkened as he studied Mia's serene expression. He knew she would be shocked if he did reveal his heart's desire. "The toast I like best is 'The Lord gives us our relatives. Thank God we can choose our friends.'"

"How true," she said in agreement. "What are you drinking?"

He raised his in a salute. "It's an Alabama Slammer."

"That's too strong for me." Her medical school roommate's brother had paid for his education tending bar at a suburban Houston catering establishment. Whenever she asked him about a particular cocktail he was able to tell her the ingredients.

A waitress approached their table, giving Kenyon a Cheshire-cat grin. "Hey, Ken. Long time no see. How's the family?"

He returned her smile. "They're good, Lisa. How is your family?"

Mia's gaze shifted from Kenyon to the petite, light-skinned woman with neatly braided extensions. She was dressed in black—shirt and pants with a red shoestring tie—the restaurant's standard uniform. She would have to be blind not to know Kenyon and Lisa had some history between them.

"The kids are getting big. Every day they ask when their

daddy's coming home, and I don't have the heart to tell them his deployment has been extended for another year. He wanted to come home, but I told him not to because it would be too hard on the kids to have him here for a short time, then he'll just have to leave them again."

Kenyon angled his head, his eyes meeting Lisa's. "Whenever you contact him again, please give him my best."

"I will." She gave Mia a professional smile. "Sorry about that. I'm Lisa, and I'm going to be your server tonight. I see that you have your drinks, but if you want anything else, then please let me know. I'll give you a few minutes to look over the menu. By the way, our specials are listed on the back."

Mia studied the menu, pleased to see a number of seafood selections among the customary beef, chicken and pork listed entrées. She gave Kenyon a sidelong glance, silently admiring his cropped hair. Without warning, his head popped up, his eyes meeting hers. They shared a smile.

"How's your drink?" she asked when she noticed he had taken only one sip.

"It's good."

"You're not much of a drinker." Her question was more a statement.

A hint of a smile played at the corners of Kenyon's strong mouth. "What else have you discerned?"

"You and Lisa have history."

"Are you always this perceptive?"

"She still has a thing for you," Mia stated instead of answering his question.

"She's married, Mia."

"When has that stopped a woman from liking a man, or

the reverse? I've known women who like dating married men."

Shifting his chair, Kenyon moved close enough to Mia where their shoulders were touching. "Have you ever dated a married man?"

She shook her head. "Never, and I hope never to become a third party in someone's marriage. They date married men because they consider them safe, see them whenever it is convenient for them, and usually it is the single person who is in control of the relationship."

Kenyon traced the outline of her ear. "Cheating can be dangerous to one's health and well-being."

Lowering her lids, Mia peered up at Kenyon through her lashes. "Have you ever cheated on a woman?"

A beat passed. "No."

"To your knowledge has a woman ever cheated on you?"

"Have had a few," he whispered, his mouth only inches from hers.

"What did you do?"

"Broke up with them."

The second hand on Mia's watch made a full revolution before she spoke again. "Did your wife cheat on you?"

"It wasn't quite that simple. The problem was we never should've married in the first place, because we rarely got to see each other. I was a pilot and she was a flight attendant. I accept the blame for assuming it would've been easy for her to adjust to life in a small town."

"Where was she from?"

"Chicago. Things were good between us whenever we had layovers in the same city, but it was the complete opposite once we were back in West Virginia. When Sam complained that she felt as if she were smothering in Jonesburg, I suggested moving to Charleston. She countered, saying she preferred Chicago. I went through a lot of soul searching, and in the end I compromised and moved."

Mia rested a hand on his back. "What happened, Kenyon?" she asked after a long, pregnant pause.

"The same way she couldn't adjust to Jonesburg, I discovered I couldn't adjust to living in a large metropolitan city. Sam made it easy to end the marriage when she came to me, admitting she'd been seeing another man. It wasn't until we were separated that she confessed to having an abortion because she hadn't known whose baby she was carrying."

Mia felt his pain as surely as it was her own when he picked up his glass and took a huge gulp. It was as if he needed the alcohol to fortify himself. "I'm so sorry, Kenyon."

Kenyon didn't want Mia to feel sorry for him, because he'd wallowed in enough self-pity to last a lifetime. "It's okay. In the end we both got what we wanted. She got to live in Chicago and I came home."

Lisa returned to take their dining orders. Mia selected Cesar salad with grilled Gulf shrimp, and Kenyon decided on broiled salmon with kale and butternut squash. Most of the dancers had returned to their tables when a live band played a slow, quiet, bluesy number that provided the perfect backdrop for leisurely dining.

It was as if the floodgates had opened, and Kenyon revealed he and Lisa had dated briefly when they were in high school. He took her to his prom and he was her date for hers. However, Lisa wanted to get married, while he'd planned to go college to major in aeronautical engineering. They parted amicably, and after graduating college he joined the air force, where he learned to fly fighter jets.

"After I left the air force I went to work for a small

domestic commercial carrier. After a year, I applied to one of the major airlines and was assigned to domestic and international routes."

"Which route did you like best?"

Kenyon leaned into her soft, scented warmth. "The one where I was able to come back to Jonesburg. I was no different than most people growing up around here. I couldn't wait to leave. That's why I opted to go to an out-of-state college."

"Where did you go?"

"MIT."

Mia giggled softly. "So, I'm dating a brainiac."

"No, it's nothing like that. I do well on exams."

"Oo-oo, it's nothing like that," Mia mimicked. "You're freaking brilliant, Kenyon."

"So are you, *Dr.* Eaton." Kenyon stressed her professional title. "Not everyone can become a doctor."

"I studied my behind off."

Kenyon winked at Mia. He found her modesty charming and refreshing. She was the epitome of beauty *and* brains, yet she tended to downplay them. "It's not how you did it, princess, but did you do it. And you did. You were able to realize your dream to become a doctor."

Pressing her forehead to his, Mia kissed the end of his nose. "Have you realized your dreams?"

His eyelids came down, shuttering his innermost feelings. "Not all of them. I left Jonesburg to attend college, but instead of returning to teach or work at an aerospace company I joined the air force. I signed up for flight school and learned to fly fighter jets. Coming home on leave was always stressful, because my mother claimed she had recurring dreams of me being shot down in combat. And it didn't help that Grandma Lily backed up her premonition."

With wide eyes, Mia stared at Kenyon. There was

something in his eyes that frightened her. "Is your grandmother clairvoyant?"

"The only thing I'm going to say is when my grandmother warns you about something—don't ignore the warning." Reaching for a napkin, Kenyon dabbed at the corner of her mouth.

"What did you do?"

"I fulfilled my military obligation, and you know the rest."

"You gave up what could have been an incredible military career, then one as a pilot, to return to your hometown to become a sheriff."

Kenyon detected derision in Mia's words and tone. "You think I made the wrong decisions?"

"No. I think you did what you needed to do for emotional and mental stability."

The wall Kenyon had erected to keep all women at a distance after he'd discovered his ex-wife's duplicity came crashing down with Mia's answer. He hadn't asked the question to validate whether he was right or wrong to give up a glamorous and exciting career as an airline pilot. He'd asked because he'd found himself falling in love with the sexy doctor. He wanted her to respect his decisions and he would hers.

"You're right."

"Are you happy, Kenyon?"

There came a beat, a moment of silence as their chests rose and fell in a syncopated rhythm. "Now that I've met you, I'm more than happy. I'm delirious."

Tears pricked the backs of Mia's eyelids, and she blinked them back before they overflowed and fell. "Stop it," she whispered.

"Stop what, Mia? Stop thinking about you? Or stop liking you?"

Picking up her napkin, she pressed it to her eyes. "All of the above," she said through the cloth.

Reaching for the napkin, Kenyon pulled it from her loose grip. "That's not going to happen. I've never been one to turn my emotions on and off like a faucet."

Eyes bright with unshed tears, Mia met his eyes. "Where are we going with this?"

"We're going home and—"

"I know we're going home," she interrupted. "What I mean is where are we going with what I assume will become a relationship?"

"What if I leave that up to you, Mia? After all, you're the transient one."

Mia felt as if she'd been doused with ice-cold water. She'd committed to practice medicine in Jonesburg for a minimum of two years, and Kenyon had called her someone just passing through. Dr. Lyman had asked whether she would be willing to take over his practice upon his retirement and she had yet to give him an answer.

It had only been a week, yet she'd connected with her patients in a way she hadn't thought possible. Treating them had become more personal than those she saw in the E.R. or the hospital's clinic. She was given the choice of reviewing their records before they came in, so it was as if she knew more about them than just their names and ages. Unknowingly, they'd become her neighbors.

"I am not a transient. Don't forget that I'll spend the next two years of my life here, and that will make me a legal resident."

"What are you going to do after you complete your residency?"

A mysterious smile parted her full lips. Mia wanted to tell Kenyon her decision to put down permanent roots in Jonesburg would depend on a particular lawman's intentions. “I don’t know,” she said instead. “I suppose it would depend on a number of things.”

“Are you at liberty to name at least one of those things?”

Looping her arms around his neck, Mia pressed her mouth to his ear and told him. Pulling back, Kenyon looked at her as if she’d suddenly taken leave of her senses. “You’re kidding, aren’t you?”

Mia sobered. “Do I look as if I’m kidding?”

He shook his head. “No.” He reached up and pulled her arms down. “Let’s go.”

Kenyon signaled for Lisa. He paid for their food while leaving her a very generous tip. Her husband had joined the reserves to supplement his income, but like so many others found themselves deployed to Iraq or Afghanistan. His regular salary stopped, leaving his family to rely solely on his military pay.

He didn’t give Mia time to react when they reached the parking lot and he picked her up and carried her to where he’d parked the Yukon. “Open the door,” he ordered when she reached into her tiny purse for the fob.

“Hey, I thought I was going to drive,” Mia protested when she found herself in the passenger seat.

“Tonight I don’t need a designated driver.” He had taken only two sips of his drink, and that meant he was alert and in complete control of all his reflexes.

Chapter 11

"Slow down, Kenyon! We're going to get stopped for speeding."

Kenyon looked at the speedometer. He was fifteen miles over the posted speed limit. "And what do you think is going to happen if I am stopped, princess?"

Mia stared at the lights on the dashboard, pondering his question. "Probably nothing."

Kenyon took a quick glance at his passenger. After she'd whispered what she'd wanted him to do to her, it was all he could do not to embarrass himself. He'd always thought himself a good judge of character, but Mia had managed to fool him not once but twice. First he'd thought her a snob until she'd explained her aloofness. Although he'd thought her sexy he hadn't and couldn't believe she would let go of the cool poise she carried around like a badge of honor. It was as if she wouldn't let anyone see her lose control. After all, doctors were taught to react calmly even during the most devastating disaster. What she'd asked him to do to her was beyond shocking. It was downright ribald.

Mia's head swiveled when she realized Kenyon has passed the turn leading to downtown Jonesburg. "Aren't we going to stop so I can pick up a change of clothes?"

"I'll stop at your place tomorrow and pick up whatever you need for the rest of the weekend."

"What about my toiletries?"

"You can give me a list of everything. And because you're so anal I'm certain I'll be able to find everything on your list."

"I'm not anal."

"You think not?" Kenyon retorted, accelerating as he sped over the railroad tracks. "Your apartment is so neat I'm willing to bet you can eat off the floors."

"And yours isn't?" she countered.

"I pay someone to clean my house. And there's not much to do except dust because I'm only there three days a week."

Mia watched trees whizz by when Kenyon increased his speed. She had to talk, say anything to keep her mind off his driving. "Don't you go a little stir crazy working, sleeping and eating in the same place for ninety-six straight hours?"

"Not really. I stay busy reading and watching television. My deputies have amassed an incredible DVD collection of movies." Initially spending that much time alone had bothered Kenyon, but after several months he'd found it comforting.

When he'd returned to Jonesburg to live he'd moved in with his parents until he found a place of his own. He wasn't back three months when the mayor appointed him acting sheriff. Not interacting with anyone left him time to think and plan what he intended to do with the abandoned dilapidated property he'd purchased for back taxes. When Samantha refused to accept a divorce settlement, Kenyon used the money to buy supplies to renovate the barn. The skills he'd learn from his grandfather were utilized when he put a new roof on the barn, divided the loft into bedrooms and installed windows to capture the stunning vistas. He'd done all of the work converting the barn for family living; the exception was the plumbing and electrical work.

Mia let out an audible sigh when he maneuvered into the driveway to his house. "See. I got you here safe and in one piece," Kenyon taunted. "Don't move. I'll help you down."

Less than a minute later they stood in the middle of the living room, staring at each other. The bravado Mia had exhibited at the restaurant had vanished like cold droplets of water on a hot griddle. What she'd asked Kenyon to do to her had come from a place so alien to her that if he hadn't reacted she never would've believed she'd made the request. The gray eyes seared her face like lasers, and she couldn't move. She felt like a hapless firefly trapped in a jar for someone's amusement.

Kenyon took a step, his hands going inside her coat and around her waist. "I won't touch you—"

Mia stopped his words when she placed her fingers over his mouth. "Shush, baby," she whispered. "I want you to touch me."

She'd told him that she wanted him to make love to her, and any further conversation she deemed redundant. At twenty-eight she wasn't afraid to say what she didn't want. And she was old enough to deal with the consequences of her actions. The first time she saw Kenyon Chandler she felt something she'd never experienced with another man—a physical attraction. Mia hadn't known whether he was married, single or a misogynist. All she knew was that she wanted to sleep with him. Kenyon's response was to sweep her up in his arms, carry her up the staircase and down the hallway to his bedroom.

Mia glanced around the enormous space, her gaze lingering on a California king-size bed with a massive carved-mahogany headboard. The eclectic mahogany furnishings commanded attention from the tall, glass-fronted secretary desk, to a country French armoire and Chinese chest. Period chairs were positioned under a round table near a set of casement windows. It was the perfect place to share morning brunch, afternoon tea or late night cordials. The bedroom reflected the personality of the man who slept there: masculine and boldly arrogant.

She didn't move when Kenyon slipped her purse off her shoulder, placing it on a tapestry-covered love seat. Her coat followed, then headband and dress. Bending slightly, he took off her shoes and pantyhose. She stood before him in a black lace strapless bra and matching bikini panties. Her clothes had hidden a slender, curvy body that was undeniably womanly. When he reached around her back, she stopped him.

"Not yet."

It was Mia's turn to undress Kenyon when she pushed him gently to sit on the tufted bench at the foot of the bed. Slowly, methodically, she pulled off his boots, her fingers faltering slightly when she encountered a small automatic in an ankle holster. She removed it, handing it to him, then continued, taking off his socks.

Kenyon gripped the edge of the bench, then closed his eyes when he felt Mia's hand travel up his inner thigh over his slacks. He hardened so quickly that if he hadn't been sitting he was certain his legs wouldn't have been able to keep him upright. He sucked in a lungful of air when she unbuckled his belt, pulling it agonizingly slowly from the loops. It landed on the floor beside his shoes and socks.

The sensations racing over his skin felt like tiny pinpricks as Mia continued to undress him. He lifted his hips slightly to aid her removing his slacks. She folded them neatly before placing them on the love seat with her coat and dress. A slight gasp echoed in the silent room when she saw his erection straining against the cotton of his boxer briefs. As a doctor she probably had lost count of the number of naked bodies she'd observed, and he'd wondered if she would be immune to his.

Mia glanced up to find Kenyon watching her reaction to his hard-on. "It's very different when I'm not examining a patient," she said, seemingly reading his mind.

Not waiting for her to finish, Kenyon reached down and pulled his sweater up and over his head. Rising to his feet, he removed his briefs and stood before her resplendent in his manly nakedness. He unhooked her bra, tossing it on the chair, then eased her panties down her curvy hips and long legs. It was only when he turned her around to press her buttocks to his groin did he see what her clothes had concealed.

Mia Eaton was full of surprises. She'd been inked. A caduceus had been tattooed at the base of her spine. Wrapping his arms around her waist, he fastened his mouth to the side of her neck. "When did you get the tramp stamp?" Her laugh was low, husky, the sound sending shivers up and down his body.

"A week after I found out I'd passed the licensing exam."

Bending her over his arm, Kenyon lowered his head and traced the outline of the staff with two entwined snakes and two wings at the top. "You just verified something for me."

"What's that?"

"You are naughty."

She laughed again. "Only at times."

"We'll see about that."

Mia wasn't given time to ponder Kenyon's cryptic statement when she found herself in his arms again and carried into the en suite bath. There was a soaking tub set into a raised platform and a shower enclosure with two showerheads.

Anchoring her arms under his shoulders, she pressed her breasts to his chest when he lowered her feet to the shower floor. The area between her legs was wet, throbbing. Her craving for Kenyon surpassed anything she'd ever felt. She sucked in her breath when a stream of cold water flowed over her head before Kenyon adjusted the temperature.

"Is it warm enough now?"

Mia nodded. She wanted to tell him she was on fire, that she needed him inside her to extinguish the flame. "Yes-s-s."

Kenyon turned on the water for his showerhead. "Why are your teeth chattering?"

"Why do you have an erection?"

He glanced down at his blood-engorged penis. "It's been like that ever since you came to town. I go to bed with a hard-on, and I wake up with a hard-on."

Mia shivered again, this time when Kenyon punched a button on a built-in dispenser with bath gel and lathered her chest with it. She closed her eyes, luxuriating in the feel of his hands tracing the outline of her breasts. "Do you do anything about it?" she whispered.

"No, because I was waiting for you."

Her eyes flew open. "You'd planned to sleep with me?"

Kenyon continued soaping her body. "No, princess. I

would never be that presumptuous. I'd prayed you would allow me to sleep with you."

Tilting her chin, Mia stared up at the man whose hands were doing incredible things to her body. Her breasts felt heavy, the nipples tightening into hard buds. The expression of carnality sweeping across his handsome features left her quaking like a leaf in a strong wind.

Her hand searched between his thighs, grasping his penis as a sense of power came to her. Kenyon's admission was an indication he'd wanted her as much as she wanted him. Going on tiptoe, she kissed his ear. "I need soap." He was washing her body and Mia wanted to return the favor.

Mia's knowledge of the human body gave her an advantage. She massaged the muscles along the back of his neck, the brachioradialis—the muscle enabling the forearm to flex on the arm—and the long palmaris—the muscle enabling various hand movements. By the time she'd worked her way between his thighs and down to his legs, Kenyon had slumped against the wall, resisting the urge to squeeze his penis to stop the rush of semen threatening to erupt. Every nerve in his body hummed like live electrical wires.

"No!"

The single word exploded from the back of his throat when Mia went down on him. His attempt to pull her hair prove futile. It was too short. Kenyon knew if he didn't extricate her from his throbbing penis he would ejaculate in her mouth—something he'd never done.

Mia anchored her arms around her lover's powerful thighs, holding on to to him as if he were her lifeline. Excitement raced through her body when he pumped his hips, keeping tempo with her suckling. When she felt the rush of semen, she stopped it by applying pressure to the large vein running along the back of his penis. She did it over and over, frustrating Kenyon until he reached down and forcibly pulled her to a standing position.

Eyes wild, teeth bared, Kenyon's fingers bit into the tender flesh on her waist. He sank down to the tiles, bringing her with him. It was Mia's turn to cry out when his mouth covered her mound; his teeth gently nipped her clitoris while his tongue simulating making love to her.

Mia's heart pounded so hard in her chest she thought she was having a heart attack. She arched her body in sheer ecstasy when an orgasm held her captive before letting her go. This was followed by another—longer and stronger than the first. They kept coming, overlapping one another until she felt herself slipping away from reality as Kenyon's growl of release echoed in her ear.

Waves of lingering pleasure throbbed through Mia when Kenyon rinsed her body, toweled her dry and carried her out of the bathroom and into the bedroom. She remembered him covering her with a sheet and several blankets, but not much else when she succumbed to the sleep of a sated lover.

Kenyon returned to the en suite bath to rinse and dry his body. He adjusted the thermostat, raising the heat, then turned off the bedside lamp. Slipping into bed next to Mia, he rested an arm over her waist, pulling her hips to his groin. She moaned softly, then settled back to sleep.

She'd asked him to make love to her—and he had. But what he hadn't expected was for her to reciprocate. What Kenyon didn't want to acknowledge was that Mia would be the first woman he would spend the entire night with since his divorce. He'd wanted her in his bed—and she was. The only thing that now remained was having her in his life—forever.

* * *

Mia opened her eyes when she felt pressure in the lower portion of her belly. Turning her head she saw Kenyon lying on his belly with his arm flung over her middle. She managed to push his arm off and slip out of bed without waking him.

Cool air swept over her naked body as she made her way to the bathroom. Everything that had happened the night before came rushing back. They'd left the Tunnel, coming back to his house. She'd undressed him and he'd reciprocated. Mia couldn't and did not want to remember all that had taken place in the shower, because it had been the first time she'd engaged in fellatio. She didn't know what had possessed her, but it seemed like a natural reaction to their lovemaking.

After opening several drawers, she managed to find a supply of cellophane-wrapped toothbrushes. Mia went through the ritual of brushing her teeth, rinsing her mouth with a spearmint dental rinse and had washed her face when she saw Kenyon's reflection in the mirror over the double sinks.

"Good morning."

He moved up behind her, pressing a kiss to the nape of her neck. "Good morning, princess. Why are you up so early?"

"What time is it?"

"It's a little after four."

She blotted the moisture from her face with a thirsty towel. "That is too early to get up." It would be a while before she would get into the habit of sleeping seven or eight hours a night like normal people.

Kenyon patted her bottom. "Why don't you go back to bed? I'll join you in a few minutes."

Mia returned to the bedroom, smoothing out the sheets

and straightening the blankets. She was in bed, lying on her side when Kenyon returned, the smell of toothpaste wafting in her nostrils. She giggled like a young child when he nuzzled her neck.

Kenyon blew his breath over the nape of her neck. "Don't tell me you're ticklish?"

"I'm not going to tell you whether I am or not because you'll use it to your advantage."

"What makes you think I'm going to take advantage of you? After all, you were the one who shocked the hell out of me when you—"

"Don't you dare say it."

Reaching over, Kenyon flicked on the lamp, then turned back to stare at Mia. "Please don't tell me you're too embarrassed for me to say that you gave me a blow job. Or, perhaps I should use the more technical terminology—fellatio."

"I am not embarrassed. After all, I am a doctor."

"Being a doctor has nothing to with it, Mia. All it means is that you've seen a lot of naked bodies. No doubt corpses as well as the live variety. What I'm referring to is the number of men you've slept with. You don't have to tell me how many, but I'm willing to bet there hasn't been more than two or three, because you couldn't have had time for a relationship with all the studying you had to do."

Kenyon didn't know how close he'd come to the truth, but Mia wasn't about to admit that to him. "I still may not have time for a relationship."

"Why not?"

"I'm only off one day a week, and starting next weekend I'll be on call."

"Don't worry, baby, we'll work something out."

Mia shifted, facing him. "Now I'm 'baby.'"

"You were always 'baby,' baby."

They shared a long, soul-searching stare. It was as if Kenyon could see behind her eyes, into her heart, to know that she was falling in love with him. Under the arrogant exterior was a man with whom she felt safe, someone she knew would protect her even when she had measures in place to protect herself.

Her heart kicked into a higher gear when his expression changed, desire darkening his eyes. The pressure of his thighs, her breasts crushed against the wall of his hard chest, his arm around her waist—tactile sensations that made it impossible for her to resist the quivering desire pulling her under.

Kenyon pulled Mia closer, their warm, moist minty breaths mingling. His gaze focused on her full lower lip before his mouth closed over hers. His teeth fastened on her lip, pulling it gently into his mouth. He alternated suckling and gently nipping her lip until it throbbed like a pulse.

She kissed him back, her tongue as busy as his when she tasted the recesses of his mouth. Rising passion thrummed through her body, and she moved sensuously against him. Kenyon stirred something in her that was so primal that it frightened Mia with its unbridled intensity. It was the very essence of his masculinity that prompted her to make love to him with her mouth—something she'd never done with another man, and the moment she had taken him into her mouth she'd realized her power and Kenyon's vulnerability.

But then he'd turned the tables, his head going between her legs, his mouth and tongue inciting a ravenous desire for more. He'd become a sexy beast and she his prey, he devouring her flesh while her whole body screamed for relief and satisfaction. And then it happened—multiple orgasms crashing over her like storm-tossed ocean waves.

Mia had believed she was going to drown in an intense ecstasy that threatened to stop her heart when suddenly the sensual storm stopped, leaving her limp, weak and unable to move. She remembered Kenyon putting her in bed, but not much else.

Kenyon kissing Mia was not enough. Kissing her and touching her had turned him on, but it was still not enough. His hands and fingers had charted a path over her silken flesh, committing the dips, curves and valleys to memory. Like a sculptor caressing his creation, he held her small, firm breasts in his hands, thumbs sweeping over the nipples where they hardened like tiny pebbles. He released her breasts, trailing fingertips down her ribs, over her flat belly and even lower to the soft down covering her mound.

"Open your legs, baby."

Her silken thighs parted, heat and moisture wrapping around his fingers, the scent of rising desire wafting in his nostrils. Everything about the woman in his bed triggered the basic instinct for every living organism—the need to mate.

And that is what Kenyon wanted with Mia. He wanted to make love to her, with her and mate. She'd complained they'd only known each a week, but he had to remind her they had met—even if they hadn't been formally introduced—more than a month before. It was enough time for him to fantasize about having her in his bed, a fantasy that had become his reality.

The flesh between his thighs stirred restlessly and then hardened so quickly he gasped audibly. Shifting, he reached over and opened the drawer to the bedside table and took out a condom from the supply he kept there. Everything appeared magnified: the whisper of Mia's breathing, his labored inhalations and exhalations, and the distinctive sound of his opening the packet and rolling the latex cylinder over his erection.

Moving over Mia, he knelt between her legs and lowered his body until their chests were touching. Kenyon kissed her hair and forehead. He pressed a kiss to her ear, along the column of her neck, lingering at the hollow to her throat, where a pulse pounded a runaway rhythm. Her arms came under his shoulders, holding on to him as the muscles in his back tightened. Mia looping her legs around his hips, her feet stroking his leg was his undoing.

Grasping his penis, he positioned it at the apex of her thighs and he eased himself into her tight body until every inch of his flesh was enveloped in warm heat. His sigh was echoed by Mia. He began to move, taking long, measured strokes, then changed rhythm when he plunged hard and fast, the satisfaction of being inside her escalating.

The pleasure was so intense Mia could hardly bear it. Kenyon's sensual assault, then his retreat, made her feel as if she was coming out of her skin while losing her mind. She arched, coming up to meet his thrusts when his hands slipped under her hips. His fingers tightened on the rounded globes of flesh, making it almost impossible for her to move when he pressed closer.

The retreat ended and he began a full-out assault, his penis sliding in and out, around and around, touching her womb. Mia tried escaping the sexual onslaught but failed. Her arms came down at her sides, hands curling into fists, and she surrendered to the waves of euphoria crashing over and shaking her entire body.

Kenyon felt Mia's first orgasm; it held him captive before letting him escape. Then came the second one, stronger than the first. They continued to come, she arched and convulsing until he, too, released himself, his body shaking uncontrollably as he threw back his head and growled, the sound reverberating in the room. He lay still, reveling in the aftermath of his still-throbbing sex.

It was as if her senses were magnified as Mia held on to her lover; the smell of their lovemaking had become an aphrodisiac that rekindled her desire for the man atop her. She smiled. He was her prince, her very sexy beast. She mumbled a slight protest when he pulled out.

Kenyon brushed a kiss over her slightly swollen mouth. "I'll be back. I have to throw away the condom."

She smiled. "Don't take too long."

He kissed her again. "Don't go to sleep until I get back."

Mia did manage to stay awake long enough for Kenyon to get back into bed, then she turned on her side, pressed her hips to his groin and drifted off to sleep. When she woke again the sun was high in the sky and Kenyon was next to her, snoring softly.

Chapter 12

Sylvia Yates-Chandler stood on the front porch, her eyes narrowing when she saw Kenyon with his arm around Mia Eaton's waist. When she'd spoken to her mother the night before and Lily had asked if Kenyon and Mia were together, she hadn't been able to give her an answer. However, if she'd waited to ask her the same question the answer would now be yes.

Unless he'd made other plans, she could always count on Kenyon coming for Sunday dinner. What she'd tried to do since he'd come back to Jonesburg to live was not interfere in her son's personal life. As an only child she'd raised him to be independent *and* a free-thinker. She never offered her opinion as to who he dated, and even when he married his flight attendant girlfriend Sylvia did not tell him she never liked her daughter-in-law.

Smiling, she tilted her chin when Kenyon leaned down to kiss her cheek and then pressed her cheek to Mia's. "Welcome."

Mia returned her warm smile. "Thank you for inviting me." The house where the Chandlers lived was a smaller version of the one where Sylvia had grown up. It was two stories instead of three, and there was only a front porch rather than a wraparound.

Sylvia's smooth brown face belied her six decades. Kenyon had shown Mia photographs he'd taken this past summer where the family had gotten together to celebrate Sylvia's big six-oh. She was taller than average, very slender and had styled her thick salt-and-pepper hair in a becoming blunt cut that required very little maintenance. She'd passed along her delicate features to her son.

Reaching into her leather tote, Mia removed a decorative shopping bag with gaily wrapped bottles of wine and a bouquet of roses in shades ranging from near purple to pure white. "I brought a little something for the table."

Sylvia peered into the bag. "How lovely, but you didn't have to bring anything."

Kenyon lifted his expressive eyebrows at the woman who'd offered him the most exquisite, unbridled love-making he'd ever known. He helped Mia out of her coat, hanging it on a coat tree in the entryway. "That's what I told her."

Mia smiled, deciding not to respond to Kenyon. "I stopped by your shop on Wednesday," she said to Sylvia, "but you were still on vacation. I was looking for something to brighten up my apartment."

Sylvia looped her arm through Mia's, leading her in the direction of the kitchen. Kenyon followed close behind them. "If you let me know what you're looking for I will set it aside for you."

"Do you have any crib blankets? My cousin is expecting a baby before the end of the month and I'd love to give her one as a gift."

"You're in luck, because I just finished one to replace the two I plan to give to Christine. I always try and keep at least one in inventory. The exception is if you want me to piece a personal quilt that tells a story."

"How long does it take for you to finish a personal quilt?" Mia asked as they walked into an ultramodern stainless-steel kitchen.

"It varies. If I machine-stitch it then I can complete it in under a week. Hand quilting can take as long as a month."

"Please don't sell any until I see them."

Kenyon took the bag from his mother, setting it on a stool at the cooking island. "Be certain to give her the family discount."

Sylvia swatted at him with a dish towel, but he managed to duck out of the way. "Go hang out with your father."

"Where is he?"

"In the family room with his eyes glued to the TV screen. I'm not certain whether he's watching football or basketball. I keep telling your father he's addicted, but he says he doesn't have a problem. His New Year's resolution was that he would give up watching televised sports, but that lasted exactly one day."

Cradling the back of her head, Kenyon dropped a kiss on his mother's hair. "Stop complaining, Mom. At least you know where he is and what he's doing. Some women never get to see their husbands because they spend their free time at bars, downing beers and fooling around with women, then come home and say they were hanging out with their boys watching a game."

Sylvia pushed out her lips. "Maybe you're right."

"Maybe?"

"Okay," Sylvia conceded. "You're right."

Kenyon kissed her again. "Consider yourself blessed

that he doesn't have season tickets to the Ravens or the Cavaliers like some dudes I know."

"That's when I serve him with divorce papers."

"And that's when there will be women lined up for at least a mile to scoop up what you tossed out."

"Nobody is getting *my* man, and that's why I know he'll never do anything as asinine as buying season tickets for *any* team."

Kenyon winked at Mia over his mother's head. "If you don't need me to help up out there, then I'm going to join Dad."

Sylvia patted his shoulder. "I'm good here. Tell your father we're going to sit down to eat in about twenty minutes."

"Can I help with anything?" Mia asked, once Kenyon left the kitchen.

"I'll get a vase and you can arrange the flowers for the table." Opening a cabinet under the cooking island, Sylvia retrieved a vase, handing it to Mia. "How do you like working with Dr. Lyman?"

"I like it a lot."

"Don't you find him gruff?"

Mia nodded as she methodically arranged the blooms according to color, beginning with the lightest and surrounding them with darker hues. "Only a little. Thankfully he doesn't yell like some the supervising doctors in the hospital where I interned."

The older woman stared at Mia as she filled the vase with water. It had only been a week, but she appeared confident and more mature than she was in Matewan. Dressed in a pair of tailored navy slacks, imported slip-ons and a white silk man-tailored shirt, the young doctor looked as if she'd planned to join her highbrow friends for afternoon tea. The single strand of pearls around her long, slender neck and a pair of matching studs completed her chic look. If nothing else, she would force the other young women to step up their wardrobes.

"I've heard good things about you, Mia."

Her hands stilled as she stared at Kenyon's mother. "You have?"

"Yes. A couple of Dr. Lyman's patients came into my shop yesterday singing your praises. I know you said you're here to complete your residency, but if you decide to leave and Dr. Lyman's retires, it will the first time in over a hundred years that Jonesburg won't have a resident doctor."

"I still haven't decided whether I'm going to take over Dr. Lyman's practice once he retires."

"Do you have a young man waiting for you back in Texas?"

A rush of heat stung Mia's cheeks. She hadn't expected Sylvia to be so candid. "No, I don't."

"All I'm saying is that you should consider staying on."

"I'll think about it."

What she didn't want to do was give anyone the false impression that she planned to stay on when she wasn't certain how in the next two weeks her life would change; meanwhile, Sylvia and Millard Lyman were pressuring her to make a commitment for two years in the future. What she found odd was that Kenyon hadn't broached the subject of her putting down roots in Jonesburg. They had shared a bed, but that didn't necessarily translate into sharing a future.

Both were consenting adults, and because they'd made love it didn't mean she was looking for a commitment. Her plan was to enjoy what Kenyon Chandler offered, and when it was over she would be left with her memories.

She walked out of the kitchen and into the dining room

and set the vase down on the table covered with a white crocheted tablecloth over a goldenrod liner. The flowers added to the elegance of china, silver and crystal at each place setting. Mia noticed that the china cabinet atop a buffet server, credenza and the living room tables all bore the same scrollwork, and she wondered if Sylvia's father had made the pieces, because Selena had mentioned that her grandfather had been a master furniture maker. It was apparent Kenyon had picked up his grandfather's talent for working with his hands. She had just returned to the kitchen when a chorus of loud groans went up from another part of the house.

"They're really into it now," Sylvia said under her breath.

"Will they leave the game to eat?"

"No game is ever *that* important. Whenever you call 'time to eat' they come running. And, remember, if the women cook then the men clean up, and vice versa."

"Kenyon cooked for me *and* cleaned up." Mia realized she'd offered too much information when Sylvia turned slowly, giving her a long penetrating stare. There was something in the way his mother was looking at her that communicated she knew they were sleeping together.

"I'm glad you and Kenyon are getting along."

"What about Mia and Kenyon?" Morgan Chandler asked, as he strolled into the kitchen. "It's halftime," he asked when his wife lifted questioning eyebrows.

Sylvia gave her husband of nearly forty years a tender smile. "He's helping her adjust to life in Jonesburg."

Morgan approached Mia, pulling her into a strong embrace. Tall, extremely attractive, with cropped silver-gray hair and powerfully built, he prided himself on staying in shape. The sparkling flecks in his hair were the perfect complement to his nut-brown complexion. He was dressed down in a pullover, jeans and running shoes.

"Good seeing you again. How do you like our quaint little town?"

Mia returned his hug. "I love it. I can walk out of my apartment and buy everything I need on a daily basis. What I can't find on Main Street I get from off the internet." She'd purchased the wine and flowers from local shops.

Morgan winked at her. "I hope you plan to stay. The last time I spoke to Millard he said he didn't know how long he's going to continue to practice."

"I'll be around for the next two years."

Kenyon walked into the kitchen, his eyes meeting Mia's. He'd overheard his father mention her staying in Jonesburg beyond her residency. He'd told himself he wouldn't mention her leaving again. What he'd planned to do was convince her to stay by courting her. Pulling his gaze away, he stared at the golden roasted turkey sitting on a large platter, its juices pooling onto the ceramic dish.

"Do you want me to start bringing the food into the dining room?" he asked his mother.

"Yes. You can take the turkey. Morgan, there's a dish of potato salad in the fridge, and Mia, there's a bowl of tossed salad on the lower shelf in the fridge. I'm going to check and see if the rolls are done."

Mia sitting on Kenyon's right and facing Morgan, spooned a portion of country-style green beans onto her plate with a slice of roast turkey, herb stuffing and potato salad. Selena said Sylvia was a better cook than Grandma Lily, and she had to concur. Never had she ever eaten turkey that literally melted on her tongue, and the Parker House rolls were to die for. The next time she spoke to Selena she would tell her she was eating more often.

"Are you certain you're not going to have coffee and

cake?" Sylvia asked Mia when she touched the corners of her mouth.

"I can't eat another morsel of food. I'll have coffee, but I'm going to pass on the carrot cake."

"What if I pack some up for you?"

"Thank you, ma'am." Three pairs of eyes were trained on Mia.

"You can call me Sylvia, Mom or Mrs. Chandler, but not ma'am. In this family *ma'am* is reserved for grandmothers. Now, if Kenyon is ready to make me a grandmother I'd be honored if you called me that again."

Kenyon draped an arm over Mia's shoulders. "What about it, princess? Are you willing to help me out and give my mother a grandchild?"

Her attempt to remove his arm proved futile. "Stop playing, Kenyon."

"I'm not playing, Mia."

"Ken, you're making Mia uncomfortable."

Kenyon stared at his father. "Please stay out of this, Dad."

Morgan glared back. "You forget this is not *your* table, son."

A pregnant silence followed Morgan's retort, a tangible uneasiness descending on the assembled. Mia wished she had the power to snap her fingers and disappear on the spot. Kenyon's arrogance had just gone off the chart. How could he embarrass her in front of his parents? She understood Sylvia's wish to claim grandmother status, because she was no different from her own mother, who was the only one in her social circle who didn't have grandchildren. Then, there had been Xavier and Denise's mother—her aunt Paulette, who'd lamented ceaselessly about not having grandchildren. Now, her prayers would be answered because Selena was carrying her first grandchild.

Kenyon cleared his throat and shattered the uncomfortable silence. "I'm sorry. What I said was not only inappropriate, but also in bad taste."

Sylvia pushed back her chair, coming to her feet, and Morgan and Kenyon followed suit. She wanted to tell Kenyon his apology should've been directed at Mia, not at everyone sitting at the table. However, she had no intention of telling him that because whatever was going on between her son and the young woman with whom he appeared enthralled, they would have to work out together.

If her mother hadn't mentioned Kenyon and Mia getting along, Sylvia wouldn't have thought of them as a couple. But when she thought back to his reaction to Mia at Selena and Xavier's wedding reception, she should've known he wasn't as unaffected by her presence as he'd pretended. He'd spent most of the time there staring at her. She noticed his distraction again during the New Year's gathering. They had been seated together, yet had reacted to each other as if they were lovers who'd had a spat. Sylvia hadn't inherited her mother's gift to predict future events, but she also wasn't so obtuse that she couldn't see what lay in front of her. Kenyon was in love with Mia Eaton. Whether Mia knew or had chosen to ignore the obvious was something she would have to deal with. And, as it was her way, Sylvia did not plan to be drawn into their personal affairs.

She'd just finished grinding coffee beans for the automatic coffeemaker when Mia joined her in the kitchen. "I'm brewing a pot of coffee, but I also have a variety of teas if you prefer tea."

Resting a hip against the countertop, Mia met Sylvia's eyes. "Coffee is okay. I'm sorry about—"

Sylvia put up a hand, stopping what she knew was an apology. "Don't, Mia. There's no need for you to apologize. If anyone should apologize to you it should be Kenyon. I've made it a practice not to implicate myself with my son and the women he chooses to become involved with. And yes, I know you are involved with him. And that's all I'm going to say."

Mia didn't know what to say, because she didn't have a comeback. She didn't know if Kenyon had told his mother they were sleeping together—something she doubted, so she had to assume it was something inherent to parents who knew more about their children than their children could've imagined.

Soon after she'd lost her virginity to someone so unworthy of the honor, Mia suspected her mother knew what had occurred. She'd kept waiting for the proverbial shoe to drop whenever Tish Eaton summoned her for a mother-daughter chat, but it never happened.

The year she'd celebrated her seventeenth birthday her mother had sat her down and told her about various forms of birth control to use *if* or *when* she became sexually active. Letitia Eaton's greatest fear wasn't her getting pregnant, but contracting an STD. Mia was able to read between the lines: her father was an ob-gyn and he could take care of any *mistake.* What Mia never told her parents was if she did find herself pregnant she would never consider terminating the pregnancy, even if she had to raise her child alone. Becoming a single mother wasn't even a blip on her radar. It was something she couldn't consider until she was at least thirty. She'd turned down Jayden's marriage proposal because she knew she wouldn't be able to juggle career and marriage. Adding motherhood to the equation would've certainly disrupted years of sacrificing thousands of hours of sleep to study and struggling to stay alert when working double and triple shifts; now that she had a coveted position working under a family doctor with more years of experience treating patients than she'd been alive, she didn't plan to have Kenyon's or any man's child until she completed her residency.

"I respect your decision, Sylvia."

"Good. Now, are you sure you don't want dessert? I can cut you a very thin slice."

"I'm sure. What I'll take is a thicker slice I can either have as a midnight snack or with my morning coffee."

Sylvia smiled. "What if I pack a few containers with enough leftovers to last you several days? I doubt if you have time to do much cooking with your busy schedule."

Mia stood straight. "The truth is I don't do much cooking because my cooking skills hover around a C-minus. I have a few cookbooks, and now that I'm not spending sixty-plus hours a week in a hospital I plan to try out a few recipes."

"I can help you out—that is, if you don't mind. Learning to cook isn't as difficult as it seems."

Mia's features became more animated as she considered Sylvia's offer. Her apartment had become her sanctuary now that the televisions she'd ordered for the living room and bedroom were delivered and connected to a cable network. She'd spent her free time in every room except the kitchen. Although she enjoyed the selections at the Kitchen, there were times when she didn't want to order takeout but cook in her own kitchen, then sit down and enjoy what she'd prepared.

"I would truly appreciate it. Of course I'd be willing to work around your schedule."

"My schedule is working from home most days. I get little or no walk-in traffic during the winter, so the shop is closed Sunday through Wednesday."

"I'm off on Wednesdays," Mia volunteered.

Sylvia grinned from ear to ear. "I guess that does it. We'll get together on Wednesdays. You have my phone number, so call and we'll arrange a time that works for both of us."

"Can you teach me how to can fruits and veggies?"

"Of course, Mia. You can put up enough jars to last you for the next three to four months. That way you'll only have to prepare a meat dish and whatever carb you want. I'll tell you when we meet again why I decided to learn canning. My mother had tried to teach me when I was younger, but I wanted no part of it. Now there isn't a summer that passes where I don't can every seasonal fruit and vegetable that exists. There's a farmer's market just outside of town that carries the most incredible fruit you've ever seen. They have peaches that are so large they look scary. Talk about sweet."

"Are they open now?" Mia asked.

"No. But come May you'll start seeing cars line up in droves for fresh berries. I load up on them for my mother, who makes preserves, jellies and jams. Selena puts them in tiny jars and offers them as samples to her new customers. She's tried to get her grandmother to make enough so she can offer them when Sweet Persuasions goes from retail to exclusively online." The two women continued to chat amicably, setting the table in the kitchen's dining area while Morgan and Kenyon cleared away the remains of dinner and packed up individual portions in storage containers.

Mia went stiff when Kenyon rested a hand on her back as they stood together at the sink. The moment ended quickly when he dropped his hand. She wasn't going to let him off that easy for embarrassing her in front of his parents.

Shifting, he moved behind Mia. "Princess," he whispered in her ear.

"Not here, Kenyon. And, definitely not now!" She'd spoken through clenched teeth. "Please move away from me."

He felt the chill radiating off her like a frigid mountain wind. Kenyon had chided himself for speaking his thoughts aloud and had apologized, so he didn't know what else was bothering Mia.

Staring out the side window, Mia sat as far away from Kenyon as the seat belt would permit her. They hadn't exchanged a word since she'd thanked him for assisting her inside his vehicle. He decelerated when reaching downtown Jonesburg, maneuvering down the street behind the rows of shops and pulling into the parking space reserved for Dr. Lyman.

She waited for him to cut off the engine, get out and come around to help her down. He reached behind her seat, grasping the handles of a shopping bag filled with leftovers. When she held out her hand for the bag, Kenyon pulled it away from her reach. Exhaling an audible sigh, Mia reached into the pocket of her coat for the key to her apartment. It was apparent he was going upstairs with her.

She unlocked the street-level door, then climbed the staircase, unlocked the door to her apartment and then pushed it open. Warmth and soft golden light from the lamp on a side table in the living room greeted her. After the massive snowstorm the temperatures had risen steadily into the mid and upper forties, and within days all traces of the white stuff had disappeared except where it had been shoveled onto grassy areas in six-foot mounds.

Turning around, she looked up at Kenyon while holding out her hand for the bag. Instead of giving it to her he walked into the kitchen and set it down on the countertop. Mia was standing near the open door, her hand resting on the knob, waiting for him to leave.

Kenyon approached her, hands shoved into the pockets of his slacks. "Close the door, Mia. I'm not leaving."

"Yes, you are."

He placed his hand over hers, forcibly closing the door. "Not until we talk."

Mia shook her head. "There's nothing to talk about. You said it all earlier today."

"I said I was sorry."

Resting her hands at her waist, she glared at him. "Apology not accepted!" She ignored his shocked expression. "I find your arrogance mind-boggling! Opening my legs doesn't give you the right to dictate what happens with my body." She opened the door again. "Thank you for a wonderful afternoon and evening, and now I'd like you to get the hell outta here!"

Kenyon knew it wasn't a goodbye but a dismissal. In a moment of madness he'd spoken the truth, said what lay in his heart and had risked losing the woman who he couldn't get out of his mind.

"I'll see you around." That said, he turned on his heel and walked out, closing the door behind him.

I'll see you around. The four words taunted Mia when she tried falling asleep, and they continued to taunt her when she sat at her table drinking endless cups of coffee early the next morning. The only time she was able to forget was when she entered an examining room to treat a patient.

Chapter 13

One day ran into the next for Mia. Dr. Lyman had returned from Charleston, but had to return two days each week because he'd agreed to become a participant in a study to test a new drug on patients with advanced RA.

In order to save time, she used a small handheld recorder to record her notes instead of writing them in the charts. At the end of the day she gave the recorder to Valerie to transcribe. The printed notes were not only easier to read but could be permanently stored in the computer's database.

It had been a month since she'd gone out with Kenyon, but in a town as small Jonesburg it was impossible not to run into each other. She was in Sylvia's shop selecting a quilt for Chandra and Preston's infant daughter when he'd stopped by during his foot patrol of the downtown area. He'd greeted her professionally as he had the other customers in the shop, then walked out without a backward glance.

Each time she caught a glimpse of Kenyon it reminded Mia how much she missed him. Not sleeping with him or sharing meals had left a void she hadn't known existed before they'd begun dating. She wanted to call and remind him that he owed her a dance, but pride had reared its ugly head, stopping her.

Sitting in her office, she spoke into the palm-size recorder. "David Facer—male, age four. Mother complained that her son didn't answer when she called his name. Left ear clear, but right had to be irrigated to soften earwax. Recommendation—a once-a-month ear wash with several drops of hydrogen peroxide, mineral oil or over-the-counter eardrops." Turning off the recorder, she placed it in an envelope for Valerie. Punching the button to the intercom, she waited for the receptionist's voice to come through the speaker.

"Yes, Dr. Eaton."

"Is David Facer our last patient?"

"Yes. Hold on, I have another call coming in. Austin Shepard needs you to come out to his place ASAP."

"Where does he live, Valerie?"

"I'll write down the address and bring it to you."

Mia ended the call, slipped out of her lab coat and checked her medical bag. She'd ordered an additional stethoscope and pediatric and adult sphygmomanometers to carry with her on house calls.

She'd put on her coat when the receptionist rushed into the office, waving a sheet of paper. Spots of color dotted her pale cheeks. Valerie Hale was one in a long line of receptionist/medical billers who had come to work for Dr. Lyman during his long career. The thirty-something divorced mother of two was dependable and efficient. She seemed immune to her boss's mercurial temperament because she needed her paycheck to supplement the paltry child support payments from her ex.

Running her hand through her highlighted chestnut waves, Valerie gave Mia the slip of paper with the information she needed to find the house. "I know you have GPS, so just put in what I have on the paper and you should be there in under ten minutes."

Mia quickly scanned what Valerie had written. "Thanks. I'll see you tomorrow."

She was out the door, bag in hand, and eight minutes after she slipped behind the wheel of her SUV she came to a stop, parking behind Kenyon's Yukon. The door to the clapboard house was ajar, and when she walked in her knees buckled slightly before she was back in control.

Kenyon sat on the floor, eyes closed, his back against a wall, holding his left arm. The sleeve of his uniform blouse was soaked with blood. It dripped off his hand, pooling on the floor. Her eyes shifted to a man sitting on a chair pointing Kenyon's nine-millimeter handgun at him. She saw movement out the corner of her eye. A thin woman with a pockmarked face stood in a corner, seemingly in shock, gripping a knife with a bloodied blade.

"Kenyon?"

He opened his eyes. "Hey, princess."

"How are you?"

"I'm good."

Her gaze returned to the man in the chair. Austin Shepard appeared to be in his late twenties. He was wearing boxers, a T-shirt and a pair of unlaced work boots. There was something about his eyes that bothered her. He had a problem focusing. Mia was willing to bet he was under the influence.

"Mr. Shepard?"

"You can call me Austin," he said, slurring. "I was the one who called Doc Lyman's office."

"Okay, Austin. I'm going to take off my coat and treat Sheriff Chandler's arm."

Austin waved the gun in her direction. "Do it, then get him the hell outta here, because then I'm gonna whup that bitch's ass. She stuck me for the last time."

"You're hurt, too?" Leaning forward, he turned slightly. The back of the T-shirt was stained with blood.

"Do you think you can put the gun down?"

"Nah. Not until the bitch puts the knife down. She cut the sheriff and I ain't gonna let her cut me again."

"Mrs. Shepard. Are you hurt?"

"Just my head when he done knock me into the wall."

"Shut up, bitch!" Austin ordered.

"I'm going to take care of Sheriff Chandler, then I'll look at you." Mia knew she didn't have time to negotiate a domestic dispute that had ended with a third party being injured. Tossing her coat on the floor, she knelt beside Kenyon, then opened her bag to remove a pair of gloves and scissors. "What happened?"

Kenyon struggled not to pass out. "She cut me when I attempted to arrest her husband because he'd beat her."

"Hold still, baby. I'm going to cut off your sleeve."

A wry smile twisted his mouth. "Now I'm 'baby'?"

"You were always 'baby,' baby," she crooned, repeating what he'd said to her what now seemed so long ago.

Working countless hours in the E.R. had steeled Mia for when she saw the deep gash in Kenyon's forearm. She whispered a prayer of thanks that Mrs. Shepard hadn't severed an artery. Kenyon had already lost a lot of blood, so her priority was to stop the bleeding. "The cut is too deep to close with Steri-Strips. I'm going to have to use sutures."

Kenyon's chest rose and fell heavily. "Just do it."

"I'm going to give you something to take the edge off the pain."

He leaned forward. "Don't give me anything that's going to put me under. I just want you to stop the bleeding," he whispered in her ear.

Mia didn't know what he intended to do, especially since he'd lost so much blood. She knew what she had to do: suture Kenyon's arm, find out the extent of Austin Shepard's wound and get Mrs. Shepard to drop the knife.

"Austin, I need you to turn on the floor lamp and bring it over here."

She waited for what seemed an interminable amount of time for the man to push himself off the chair and stumble over to the lamp. It took several attempts, but he flicked it on and pulled it as close as the cord would permit. With wide eyes, she stared at the widening stain on his shoulder blade.

Working quickly, she cleaned away the blood flowing from a three-inch gash in Kenyon's arm. Opening a package containing a sterile traumatic needle with sutures, she drew it through his flesh. Kenyon went still with each prick of the needle, exhaling audibly as she sutured the cut. Mia finished and didn't have time to admire her handiwork when she covered the sutures with sterilized gauze and a waterproof dressing. Instead of injecting him with a painkiller, Mia gave him an antibiotic. She shuddered to think of the amount of bacteria on the knife blade.

Stripping off her gloves, she slipped into a fresh pair. Austin had slumped in the chair, his legs twitching, and Mia couldn't tell whether he'd passed out or had come down off his high. Her gaze swept around the room. Kenyon's gun belt, jacket and walkie-talkie were on the floor several feet from where Austin was sprawled, the gun clenched tightly in his hand. If she could get the gun away from him, then it would be easy for her to get his wife to release the knife. However it ended, one or both Shepards were going either to jail or to the hospital.

She shook Austin's knee. "Austin, I need you to turn around so I can look at your shoulder." His rummy eyes opened and he looked at her as she had two heads. He smiled and it was then she saw his teeth. He had what she recognized as a "meth mouth." The Shepards were abusing methamphetamine.

He shifted on the worn chair, then without warning trained the powerful handgun on his wife. "If you move I'm going to kill you."

"No you're not," Mia said quietly, as she pressed her gun against the back of his head. "Drop it or I'll blow your brains out."

"Don't you hurt my man!" Mrs. Shepard screamed.

"I will hurt your man, then I'm going to hurt you, Mrs. Shepard," Mia threatened. She leaned closer, increasing the pressure against his skull. "Put the gun in your left hand, then hand it to me over your shoulder," she whispered in his ear. Austin complied, and she held it behind her back. "Kenyon, can you get up?"

"Yes, princess." His disemboweled voice floated somewhere behind her.

"You can call for backup now. And, you can also come and get your weapon."

Kenyon came to his feet, the pain in his arm intensifying as he approached Mia, who still held her automatic to the back of Austin's head. He took the nine-millimeter from Austin's loose grip and then bent over to get his radio. At that moment Jennifer Shepard sprang from the corner, right arm raised with the knife coming straight for Mia.

A single shot rang out and the knife clattered to the floor. Jennifer stopped, eyes wide and slumped to the floor.

"You shot my Jenny!" Austin cried.

"No, Austin. I didn't shoot Jenny. I shot the knife out of her hand. She fainted."

"She's alive, she's alive," he babbled over and over, tears trickling down his face.

"You forget I'm a doctor. I try to save lives, not take them. Now, hold still while I look at what your sweet Jenny did to you."

By the time Mia cleaned and covered the cut with Steri-Strips and injected Austin with an antibiotic the house was crowded with state police. Jenny was revived, handcuffed, charged with attempted murder and read her rights before she was taken away, sobbing uncontrollably. Austin was also arrested for holding an officer hostage, and was taken away with his wife. The knife was placed in an evidence bag.

Kenyon, who'd given the arresting officers a detailed account of what had happened after he'd responded to the call from Austin Shepard, asked that they conceal the fact that Dr. Eaton carried a registered handgun in her medical bag. His arm hung limply at his side as he tried staying upright, making eye contact with Mia.

Beckoning to one officer, Mia leaned close to him with his approach. "Sheriff Chandler has to go to the hospital. He's lost a lot of blood."

The youthful-looking officer lifted his shoulders. "He refused when we told him we were going to transport him to the hospital."

"He needs at least a unit of blood," Mia insisted.

"I'm sorry, Doc, but we can't force him to go."

Exasperated, she went in search of one of Kenyon's deputies. She found both flanking him on the sofa. "I need one of you to take the sheriff in his truck and drive him back home. Then, I'm going to need your help getting him into bed."

Deputy Eddie Field took charge. "I'll drive him back. Steven, we're going to have to cover for Kenyon until he's cleared to return to duty." He nodded to Mia. "We're ready whenever you are, Doc."

Mia had stored the used medical supplies in a bag stamped Medical Waste, placing it and the handgun in her medical bag. She'd given the police her statement and contact information in case they needed to reach her. Walking out the house, she breathed in a lungful of cool, nighttime mountain air. Out in the country the stars looked closer, brighter. West Virginia was spectacular in the winter and she tried imagining the lush splendor of the forests, deep valleys, gorges and waterfalls in the spring and summer. She'd fallen in love with her new state, *and* she was also in love with Jonesburg's sheriff.

"Thank you, Deputy Field, I'll take it from here." Mia had instructed Eddie Field and Steven Powell to carry Kenyon up the staircase and place him on his bed. Eddie had removed Kenyon's shoes, socks and uniform pants, while Steven placed his boss's equipment on the bench at the foot of the bed.

Eddie lowered his eyes. "Please call me Eddie."

She nodded, smiling. "Okay, Eddie. Thank you for everything."

Steven, who had recently completed his police training at the state police academy, shook his head. "No, Doc. We thank you for saving Kenyon's life."

Mia stared at the two deputies. It was apparent they were quite fond of their superior officer. "You should put in a good word for Austin, because if he hadn't called my office there is the possibility that Kenyon may have bled to death."

Eddie tunneled his fingers through bright red hair as he checked his watch. "We're going to leave that up to Kenyon and the judge. We have to leave now. One of us has to cover the station house."

"Dr. Eaton, do you want us to contact Kenyon's folks?" Steven asked, as Mia led them down the staircase to the front door.

"No. I'll call them," Mia replied. She knew the call coming from her rather than the police would be less traumatic for the Chandlers. Waiting until the men left, the sound of their tires spewing gravel fading into the night, she took out her cell and tapped the speed dial for Sylvia, who answered after the second ring.

"Sylvia, Mia. I'm at Kenyon's house. I just treated him for a knife wound. Don't panic," she said softly when Sylvia's gasp came through the earpiece. "He's going to be all right."

"We're on our way."

Mia ended the call, and then retraced her steps. Somehow she had to convince Kenyon that he should go to the hospital, even if he were kept overnight for observation. Stitching him up in a nonsterile environment wasn't ideal, but necessary given the circumstances. She'd encountered two meth heads whose intent was to kill each other, while the man who'd sought to either mediate or diffuse the situation ended up losing blood from a gaping knife wound.

Walking into the bedroom, she saw Kenyon lying on his back, arms outstretched. Moving closer to the bed, she realized he wasn't sleeping. "How are you feeling?"

Closing his eyes, Kenyon drew in a deep breath. "My arm is on fire."

Mia opened her bag. "I don't care what you say, but I'm going to give you something for the pain."

"I told you before that I don't want it."

"It's not what you want, Kenyon. It's what you need. There's no honor in suffering in silence." Working quickly, she swabbed his hip, then plunged the needle into a muscle. "Your parents are coming over, but you'll probably be asleep by the time they get here." She didn't tell him that she would wait another four hours, then give him another dose of antibiotics to counter whatever bacteria had invaded the wound.

"I should've never turned my back on her," he slurred. "It's my fault that she cut me."

Leaning down, Mia kissed his forehead. "It's not your fault. Now, relax and try to get some sleep."

Covering him with a sheet and lightweight blanket, she adjusted the thermostat, left on a wall sconce and walked out of the bedroom. The sound of a car door closing resounded loudly in the stillness of the night as she made her way to the front door. She opened the door before the Chandlers could ring the bell. Sylvia's eyes were red and puffy, an indication that she'd been crying.

"Please come in. If you go up to see him now Kenyon will probably be alert enough to talk to you. I gave him something that will help him sleep through the night."

Mia found herself in Sylvia's arms, then Morgan's, as they whispered prayers of gratitude. She sat down on a chair in the living room as the Chandlers raced up the staircase to the second floor. Sandwiching her hands between her denim-covered knees, she said her own silent prayer that no one had been seriously injured or, even worse, killed. She'd encountered situations where people were murdered by someone in drug-fueled rages that not only shattered families but neighborhoods, when the police were forced to shoot and kill the person wielding a knife or gun. Would she have shot Jennifer Shepard if she'd continued to attack her? Probably. A bullet to the knee would've dropped her where she stood. Would she have killed her? Definitely not. Her uncle had trained her to shoot to disarm or disable, unlike a sniper who'd been trained for *one shot, one kill.*

Mia lost track of time as she sat waiting for the Chandlers' reappearance. It had been nearly a month since she'd talked to Kenyon, and their reunion was because of a life-and-death situation. She'd replayed their last encounter over and over in her head, wondering if perhaps she'd blown it out of proportion, if she should've accepted Kenyon's apology with a promise it would not be repeated. Then, the other voice in her head said she had a right to say what she'd said, that Kenyon had put her on the spot with his parents, leading them to believe there was more to their relationship than just sleeping together.

For her, sleeping together did mean it was serious, or it would lead to children. Did she want children? Yes. But, she also wanted to be married when she had her children. She treated too many single mothers with children, and not only did they have to encounter financial hardship but also emotional hardship. They had to be both mother and father, and the impact was overwhelming when she had to juggle working and caring for her children. There were mothers who had to wait until the weekend before they were able to bring their sick children to the E.R. or the hospital clinic because if they took off from work they'd lose a day's pay.

Mia believed children weren't things people had because it would ensure a part of themselves would live on for future generations, but the result of a very intimate and intense love for a lifelong partner. When she married she wanted it to be forever. Eatons tended to marry for life. The exception was Raleigh Eaton, who'd recently married for the fourth time. Whenever they received a wedding invitation from Raleigh the rest of the family typically did not send back their response cards until the deadline, because they never knew if Raleigh would back out of the wedding.

Slumping in the chair, Mia crossed one leg over the opposite knee and stared at the toe of her boot. Why, she mused, was she thinking about marriage and children? Did she love Kenyon? Yes. Enough to marry him? At that moment she wasn't certain. She came to her feet when she heard footsteps and voices. Sylvia was holding on to her husband's arm, smiling.

"He's asleep," Morgan said in a deep, quiet voice. "I don't how we can thank you—"

"There's no need to thank me," Mia interrupted. "I did what I've been trained to do."

Sylvia's eyebrows lifted a fraction. "Is disarming someone hopped up on drugs a part of your training?"

A rush of heat swept over Mia's face. "My uncle, who is a firearms expert, taught me to shoot. I don't advertise that I carry a handgun with me when I go out on house calls, but this time I'm glad I had it and no one got hurt as a result."

Morgan lowered his head and dropped a kiss on Sylvia's hair, the gesture reminding Mia of Kenyon. "Ken says you're a modern-day Annie Oakley."

Mia grimaced. "I don't want people to know that I have a gun."

"And they won't," Morgan countered. "Ken said the report will state that you used his off-duty weapon to disarm Jenny Shepard. I'm going to take Sylvia home where she can pack a bag. She'll stay with Ken until he can get up and do for himself."

"I'll stay tonight," Mia volunteered. "I want to monitor his vitals," she added when the Chandlers looked shocked by her offer. "I don't have office hours until ten tomorrow." She smiled at Sylvia. "If you come by at nine that will give me time to get back to my place and change before I start seeing patients."

The Chandlers exchanged a look. "Okay," Sylvia said. "If there's any change in his condition you will call me."

"Of course."

Sylvia came over and hugged Mia. "My son is in love with you," she whispered in her ear. "I'll see you tomorrow," she said loud enough for Morgan to hear.

Morgan hugged and kissed Mia's cheek. "Good night, Pistol-Packin' Mama."

Mia rolled her eyes. There was no doubt the news about her shooting prowess would spread through Jonesburg like a wildfire. The only consolation was people would believe she'd used Kenyon's gun rather than her own. His off-duty automatic was the same caliber as the one she carried, so the story was plausible.

She waited for the Chandlers to leave, then punched in the security code, arming the system. Kenyon had given it to her when they'd reached the house, otherwise she would've instructed Eddie and Steven to bring him to her apartment. Climbing the staircase for the last time, she walked into the bedroom she'd slept in the first night she'd come to Kenyon's home. Stripping off her clothes, she brushed her teeth, then stood under the spray of the shower as if the water could wash away the images of the frightening domestic violence, and if it had escalated, she could have watched the man she loved bleed to death.

Reaching for a bath sheet, she patted the moisture

from her body before slathering on a moisturizer from the supply on a shelf. She wrapped another towel around her body and, walking on bare feet, made her way into Kenyon's bedroom. Opening and closing drawers, she finally found what she'd been looking for. Pulling the T-shirt over her head, she dimmed the wall sconce, then crawled into bed next to Kenyon. He didn't move. The sedative had taken effect.

Mia put an arm around Kenyon's shoulders, easing him into an upright position, while she rearranged the pillows behind him. She'd gotten up early, put her clothes in the washer and was dressed by seven. She'd admit her cooking skills were limited, but she managed to make a light breakfast of orange juice, buttered wheat toast and soft scrambled eggs.

She handed him a cloth, watching as he washed his face. "You can brush your teeth after you eat."

Kenyon stared at the food on the tray Mia had placed on his lap. He closed his eyes, fighting the urge not to go back to sleep. Whatever she had given him the night before had to be something vets used on large animals to put them under.

"Do you mind feeding me?"

Mia wanted to remind Kenyon he was right-handed and it was his left arm that was injured but held her tongue. This was a side of the arrogant man she'd never seen, and for some reason she found it charming. "Of course not."

Sitting on the side of the bed, she picked up a fork and fed him the eggs. Breaking the toast into pieces, she placed them into his mouth, watching as he chewed and swallowed. "Your mother is coming over to stay with you."

"When are you coming back?"

"I'll be back during my lunch break," Mia promised.

"I'm going write a script for the pain, and another for an antibiotic just in case there were some nasty little germs on that knife. When was the last time you got a tetanus shot?"

"I don't remember."

"If that's the case, then you're going to get one this morning."

"You like sticking me with needles, don't you?"

"No, I don't. If you haven't had a tetanus booster in the last five years, then it's a good idea to have one within twenty-four hours of an injury." Mia met the large gray eyes ringed with long black lashes. "I didn't save your life to lose you because you're afraid of needles."

Kenyon stared at Mia, wanting to believe she cared about him and not because he'd become her patient. "Did my mother teach you to make eggs like this?"

"No. I told you I can make a decent breakfast."

"My mother told me you are a quick study, and that you know the entire canning process." Smiling, she nodded, the demure gesture making Kenyon's heart turn over in response. "What went wrong with us, princess?"

Mia picked up the glass of juice and put it to his mouth. "Drink. You're going to have to drink a lot of liquids to replenish the blood you lost."

At another time Kenyon would've pressed Mia to give him an answer. But, now it was different. They weren't together and she wasn't obligated to him in any way. She'd saved his life, and for that he would be eternally grateful. The Native Americans had a belief if someone saved your life then you were linked forever. She'd saved his life and he wanted her in his life.

"I'll follow your orders because I need to get back to work."

"No, Kenyon. It's going to be a while before you're going to be able to return to work."

"When is that?"

"I don't know," Mia said. "It all depends on how quickly you heal. Barring an infection, I estimate a couple of weeks."

"A couple of weeks!"

"Did I stutter, Kenyon?"

He blinked, then stared at her in what had become a stare-down. A smile tilted the corners of his mouth. He'd trained what he termed his lethal stare on men who were taller and outweighed him by at least fifty pounds and they had backed down. But not Mia.

"No, princess. You did not stutter."

Picking up a napkin, she touched it to his mouth. "That settles it. You will not return to duty until I give you medical clearance. Your dressing is waterproof, so if you want to take a shower, then I'll help you."

"I think I can shower on my own."

"Okay. I'll change the bed while you're in the shower. I'm going to leave a list of dos and don'ts for your mother. There's no reason why you shouldn't be ambulatory but don't overdo it. And don't forget to increase your intake of liquids."

"Yes, Dr. Eaton."

Mia picked up the tray, pleased that Kenyon had eaten everything. "I'll stop in and check on you during lunch, and I'll be back tonight to change your dressing."

"Are you…"

"Am I what?" she asked when he didn't finish his question.

"Nothing."

Kenyon was going to ask Mia whether she planned to sleep over, but changed his mind. If she wanted to stay, then she would. If not, then she wouldn't.

Chapter 14

Mia felt the heat from Kenyon's hot gaze on her when she swabbed the sutures with an antiseptic, then covered it with gauze and a waterproof bandage from the surplus in her office. It had been three days since she'd treated his arm, and she had since made several house calls to check up on him. What she hadn't done was stay over after the first night. Their eyes met and they shared a smile.

"You're healing nicely."

"When do you think you're going to remove the stitches?" They were beginning to itch, and Kenyon had to stop himself from scratching the area.

"Maybe in another week."

"That's another week of me going stir-crazy. It wouldn't be so bad staying home if I could work on the extension." He rolled down his shirtsleeve. Mia brushed his hand away, buttoning the cuff. "What are you doing for lunch?"

Mia gathered a handful of instruments and put them

in a sterilizer. "I'll probably order something from the Kitchen."

"Let's go, princess. I'm taking you out to lunch."

Mia took off her white jacket, draping it over the back of her chair, while Kenyon held her ski jacket. She slipped her arms into the sleeves. "I have to be back in time for my next patient."

"What time is that?"

She smiled at him over her shoulder. "Two."

"It's only eleven forty-five. I'll have you back with time to spare."

They walked out together. Mia waved to Valerie, who sat at her desk behind a counter talking on the phone. Kenyon waited until they were on the brick-lined pedestrian mall, then reached for her hand.

"How you feeling, son?" an elderly man called out, as he headed into the bank.

"I'm feeling much better, thank you."

When the story appeared in the local paper, all available copies were snapped up like Super Bowl tickets. Mia had to suffer through patients wanting to talk about what had happened at the Shepards rather than their ailments.

A member of the local chamber of commerce delivered a plant to the office, and the Chandlers gave her an exquisite bouquet with a note expressing their gratitude for all she'd done for Kenyon. Mia wanted to tell them she'd taken an oath to treat the ill to the best of her ability, and the plants, flowers and accolades were unnecessary.

Kenyon held open the door to the Kitchen, and when she walked in everyone stood and applauded. Whistles and catcalls joined the clapping when Kenyon lowered his head and captured her mouth in an explosive kiss that left Mia struggling to breath. The kiss only lasted seconds, but for her it seemed a lifetime. Eddie approached her, pinning a star on her jacket and declaring her an honorary deputy sheriff.

Mia laughed, burying her face against Kenyon's shoulder. There was no doubt he was in on the stunt. "I'm going to get you for setting me up," she whispered.

Cradling her to his chest, he kissed her hair. "Get me how?"

"Don't worry. I'll think of something," she promised.

Looping an arm around her waist, Kenyon led Mia to an empty table. He took her jacket and hung it up with his on a wall lined with hooks. He didn't know how she did it, but she managed to look incredibly chic in a light blue chambray shirt, jeans and boots.

"It's going to be hard for you to leave Jonesburg now that you've become a local hero," he said when he sat opposite her.

"Who said I was leaving?" Mia asked.

He leaned closer. "What about when you complete your residency?"

"I'm still not leaving. I've decided to stay on and take over Dr. Lyman's practice."

Shock and confusion assailed Kenyon as he attempted to process what Mia had revealed. "What made you change your mind?"

A mysterious smile softened her mouth, bringing his gaze to linger there. "There are a few variables."

He remembered asking her about her variables and she'd whispered that it would depend on his lovemaking. "Are you at liberty to tell me what they are?"

"I've grown quite fond of my patients."

"What else, princess?"

"I like Jonesburg. The people are warm and friendly, and it's a wonderful place to live and raise a family. There is also a certain sheriff who just happens to be slightly banged up at the present time that I've also grown quite fond of."

Kenyon waved away the waitress who'd approached their table. He didn't want or need any distractions or interruptions now that he had gotten Mia to open up to him. "I'd like you to know that that slightly banged-up sheriff is in love with Jonesburg's lady doctor."

Mia's eyelids fluttered wildly. She couldn't believe Kenyon Chandler had selected a public place to tell her he loved her. "Kenyon," she whispered hoarsely.

"Mia," he whispered, mimicking her.

"I…I didn't know. I'm shocked." She was babbling like an idiot, and her words and thoughts were tumbling over one another. "I'm sorry. I don't know what to say."

"You don't have to say anything. I just want you to know how I feel about you."

"And you should know how I feel about you. Can you stop by my place around eight?"

Kenyon didn't know whether he'd opened Pandora's box when he'd admitted to Mia that he loved her, but he knew the day of reckoning was at hand. He could either continue to fantasize about a future with Mia Eaton or exorcise her from his head and heart completely. He was emotionally prepared to accept her decision to pick up where they'd left off, or to go their separate ways to live separate lives.

"I'll see you at eight."

Mia picked up the plastic-covered menu, studying the luncheon selections. She'd always tried to eat healthy, but this was one time when she decided to throw caution to the wind. "I think I'm going to have the Kitchen Sink."

With wide eyes, Kenyon stared at Mia as if she'd asked for a glass of hemlock. "You're going to eat a hamburger?"

She laughed softly. "Yes. Why?"

"You told me you never eat burgers."

"I said I don't eat burgers because the last one I ate was concocted from some sort of mystery meat. I knew it was meat, but it looked and tasted unrecognizable."

"I can assure you that if it says beef on the menu, then it is beef. Are you going to eat the French fries and onion rings, too?"

"Yes."

Leaning back in his chair, Kenyon crossed his arms over his chest. "You are truly a chameleon. Just when I think I've figured you out, you go and change up on me."

Mia scrunched up her nose. "I'm really not that complicated. What I am is very adaptable."

"Like wearing flannel and jeans instead of silk and cashmere."

"Don't knock the silk and cashmere until you've worn them. There's nothing more luxurious against bare skin than silk."

He winked at her. "I'll remember that the next time I buy a woman a sexy nightgown."

"You buy women lingerie?"

"Occasionally."

Mia's expression didn't reveal the swell of jealousy rising in her throat and making swallowing difficult. "I've never bought men's underwear, so you have one up on me."

"Silk boxers are nice."

"Is that a hint or a suggestion, Kenyon?"

Kenyon winked at Mia again. "Both."

She returned his wink. "I'm sorry to end this very engaging conversation, but I have to order because I don't want to be late for my patient."

Kenyon signaled for the waitress, gave her their orders, then settled back to watch Mia as she stared out the plate glass window. In eight hours he would come face-to-face with his destiny. And at that time he would discover if it would be bitter or if it would be sweet.

Mia's head popped up when she heard a knock on the door.

"Hello, Dr. Eaton."

Shrieking, she jumped up and came around the desk. Standing in her office was the last person she'd expected to see. "Jayden! What a wonderful surprise. What are you doing here?"

"I flew in last weekend for my sister's wedding, then decided D.C. isn't that far from Jonesburg, West Virginia, so I decided to rent a car and drive down to see my almost fiancée."

Going on tiptoe, she threw her arms around his neck and planted a noisy kiss on his mouth. He must have asked Valerie not to announce him, because anyone who came to see her had to be announced and buzzed in by the receptionist.

Mia closed her eyes for several seconds, and when she opened them she stared at the man who had been her lover *and* mentor. He looked different, more mature, and she attributed that to the mustache and goatee. Jayden wasn't as handsome as he was attractive. His light-brown skin tended to burn if exposed to too much sunlight, and the sprinkling of freckles across his nose and cheeks had always made him look boyish.

"I shouldn't have to remind you that we were never engaged, Jay."

"I know. That's why I said *almost* fiancée."

Taking his hand, Mia pulled him to the chair, while she sat on the corner of the desk. "Please sit down. How's Denver?"

Jayden cradled Mia's hands, his thumbs moving over

her smooth knuckles. "Denver is great. But it would be even better with you there."

Mia snatched her hands away as if his were hot coals. "Did you come here to say hello or try to convince me to come to Denver?"

"Both, Mee-Mee."

She shook her head. "I'm sorry, Jayden, but I can't leave Jonesburg."

"Why?"

"I'm surprised you're asking me that," she countered, her voice rising slightly. "I'm committed to completing my residency here."

"You can complete it in Denver. The hospital is rated one of the best hospitals west of the Rockies, and everything is state-of-the-art."

"Unlike Jonesburg?"

Jayden reached for her hands again, but she shoved them in the large pockets of her lab coat. "I'm not saying that, Mia."

"Exactly what are you saying?"

"You need to be in a hospital where you can make a name for yourself. Not only are you a good doctor, but you're also a brilliant one. Your medical school grades and the score you received to get your license bore that out. You're working in a place where the main street is only a couple of blocks. You're wearing a lab coat that doesn't have your name and title stitched on it. And look at you. You're a beautiful woman, but no one would ever know it with you wearing clothes that someone living in the backwoods would wear." He grunted. "No makeup, short hair. Are you trying to prove to these people that you're one of them?"

Mia's hands tightened into fists when she wanted to slap the supercilious smirk off Jayden's face. He'd come from a long line of doctors who all lived in exclusive conclaves and sent their children to exclusives schools; when she had become involved with Jayden she'd thought he was different, but apparently she was wrong, or maybe he was a better actor than she could've imagined he'd be.

"When you asked me to marry you I vacillated for days, because although I believed I loved you I knew in my heart that I wasn't in love with you. There was something missing, and I wasn't able to figure it out until now. You're a doctor, but you have no heart. For you it's all about being in the spotlight. You chose me because my father is a doctor, and with my family's pedigree you thought it would make me the perfect wife." She stood up, her eyes flashing fire and rage. "I'm sorry you took a detour to Jonesburg, because I wouldn't marry you if you were the last man on the face of the earth. I've found someone here in Jonesburg who loves me, Jayden. He loves all of me, with the short hair, without makeup, and he's charmed by my backwoods style of dress. And the wonderful part is that I love him, and I'm going to tell him that tonight and every night of my life if he decides he wants me for his wife *and* the mother of his children. I will complete my residency, take over this practice and live out my destiny with people who don't judge others by what they look like, but what is in their hearts. Now, I'm going to ask you leave, and I hope you have a safe trip back to Denver."

"Bravo!" boomed a deep voice in the doorway.

Mia turned to see Millard Lyman in the doorway. He was actually grinning, and it was apparent he'd overheard everything. "Dr. Lyman."

Entering the small office and crossing his arms over his chest, Millard pushed his misshapen hands under his armpits. He gestured with his head. "Who is this jackass?"

Mia was tempted to laugh in Jayden's face when shock

paralyzed his features. "This *gentleman* is Dr. Jayden Wright, a trauma surgeon from Denver, Colorado."

Millard angled his head. "I'd shake your hand, Dr. Wright, but I wouldn't want to contaminate you with a microorganism I picked up from a backwoods patient." Bushy eyebrows lowered over a of pair deep-set dark eyes. "Yes, Dr. Wright, I heard what you said about my partner, and I really don't appreciate you coming in here talking to her with your so-called elitist attitude."

Jayden stood up and squared his shoulders. "No disrespect, Doc, but—"

"It's Dr. Lyman to you, son. I was a doctor before you were even an afterthought."

A rush of color spread over Jayden's cheeks, his freckles standing out in contrast. "I'm sorry, Dr. Lyman, but I don't believe Mia needs you to defend her. She has a father."

Mia gasped, shocked that Jayden had come back at the older doctor like a rabid dog. "Jayden!"

"Maybe I should call her boyfriend and have him lock your fancy ass up for harassing her. Folks in Jonesburg are funny about outsiders messing with their own. You have exactly two minutes to walk out of here, or I'm calling the law."

Jayden's eyes shifted between Dr. Lyman and the woman who'd just shattered his dream to marry a woman whose family pedigree equaled his. "Is this really what you want, Mia?"

Raising her right arm, she looked at her watch. "Go back to Denver and save a life. You now have ninety seconds, Dr. Wright."

"Good luck with your new life," Jayden spat out. He gave Mia a withering glare, then walked out of the office without a backward glance as Mia and Millard shared a smile.

"What made you take up with that jackass?" Millard asked, his smile becoming a scowl.

"Honestly, I don't know. I suppose I didn't see him for who he actually was until now. I'm not sorry he acted out this way because we probably would've remained friends and maybe I would've second-guessed myself because I'd decided not to marry him."

"I doubt that, Mia."

A look of confusion crossed her face. "Why would you say that?"

"That idiot can't hold a candle to Kenyon even if he gave him a two-mile running start. You're a local heroine, Mia, but you're also the envy of every single woman in Jonesburg because you managed to snag the most eligible of bachelors. Kenyon Chandler is one of our best and brightest who left but came back to make our town a better place. That wife he had was some piece of work. Your friend who just walked out could be her male counterpart. She hated living in Jonesburg and wasn't shy when she told anyone who would stand still long enough to listen to her. When Kenyon returned after his divorce we all held our breath, waiting for him to pack up and leave again. But fate stepped in when the sheriff resigned to save his marriage, and the mayor appointed Kenyon as acting sheriff because he had military experience and, as a federal flight deck officer, he was as accurate with a firearm as a military sniper. When it came time for him to run for the position, he ran unopposed. You know the rest."

"Why are telling me this, Millard?"

He smiled a smile that did not reach his eyes. "Don't blow it, Mia. Jonesburg is small and there's not much you can hide around here. There's talk of seeing Kenyon's vehicle parked behind the office on the weekends. There's also gossip about the two of you shopping in the Wal-Mart off the interstate and hanging out together at the Tunnel. There's no place you can go in Mingo County where someone won't recognize Jonesburg's sheriff and resident doctor."

Mia lifted her chin and her eyebrows. "You're saying this to say what?"

"Do what most young folks do. Marry, have children and live a wonderful life. You'll have a practice that runs itself, and you'll have a babysitter who'll love your babies as much as you will."

"Sylvia Chandler."

"The one and only. And if you have a boy, then you can count on Morgan teaching him to fly-fish. We used to go fly-fishing up near the rapids off Boone Lake before my hands got so bad. A couple of days before the Fourth we'd go fishing for trout and big-mouth bass for the annual Independence Day barbecue and fish-fry celebration held in the town square. There's always a lot of food, music, dancing and rides and games for the kids."

Mia felt a warm glow flow through her, knowing she had made the right decision to put down roots in Jonesburg. She woke and went to bed without the angst she'd experienced in Texas, and she had fallen in love with a man who loved her with or without haute couture and makeup.

"Aren't you being a little premature when you talk about Sylvia becoming my mother-in-law?"

"No, Mia. I'm more than twice your age and I've delivered more babies than I can keep track of. There are times when I'm wrong about something, but not too often. The first day I met you when you'd come into the Kitchen and Kenyon came over to the table, I saw something pass between you that went beyond your cousin marrying his cousin."

Mia remembered it was the weekend she'd come to Jonesburg and was forced to spend the night with Kenyon because her apartment wasn't heated. What, she wondered, had Dr. Lyman detected when they hadn't yet slept together?

"Oh."

"Yes, oh. Now, why don't you get out of here and go check on your boyfriend?"

"I still have to see Mr. Rowan."

Millard gave her a look. "I'll see Mr. Rowan. I'm going to talk him into letting me check his prostate. I believe he would prefer me poking around in him than a young thing like you. He might get so excited you'd have to use the defibrillator to restart his heart."

"Millard!"

He waved a hand. "Go. It's Friday night, and that means it's date night. As soon as I'm finished here I'm going to take the missus to dinner and then to the movies."

Mia decided to take advantage of Millard's generous offer to leave early. She had asked Kenyon to come to her apartment at eight, because she had planned something that would change their future—their destinies.

Kenyon climbed the staircase, instinctually knowing Mia would be waiting for him at the top. A smile parted his firm mouth when he saw her there. His smile grew wider when his gaze lingered on her long, bare smooth legs and narrow feet in a pair of slingback stilettos, then moved up to a black pencil skirt, wide black patent leather belt and a white transparent blouse. He would have to be blind not to see she wasn't wearing a bra under the revealing fabric.

He swallowed a groan when he wanted to hold his groin to conceal the instantaneous erection. When Mia had invited him to her apartment his mind had conjured up a number of scenarios ranging from his seducing her to standing and fighting for her.

Kenyon had taken and given orders when he served in the air force, and with his discharge he'd believed he'd left that world behind. When Mia asked whether he would come to her apartment at eight it actually hadn't been a request, but an order. And, although she'd admitted to being fond of him, that didn't mean she felt the way he did. Sam had told him she loved him and would love him until death, yet that hadn't stopped her from sleeping with another man. Then she'd compounded her deception with the revelation that she may have gotten rid of his child. Fool me once, shame on you. Fool me twice, shame on me. That had become his mantra when it came to the opposite sex.

"You look…unbelievably sexy."

Mia opened the door wider. "You think?"

Kenyon took a step, his chest brushing hers. "I know. Are you going to invite me in, or do you plan on seducing me out in the hall?"

"What makes you think I'm out to seduce you, sweet prince?"

Lowering his eyes, he saw that her nipples had hardened. "Because you're dressed for a night of seduction."

Stepping aside, Mia extended a hand. "Please come in."

Kenyon walked, his eyes widening when he saw dozens of lighted candles in the semidarkness of the living and dining area, where the table was set for two. The hauntingly melodious voice of Sting coming from a speaker singing "When We Dance" filled the apartment. He set the decorative shopping bag with a gift wrapped box inside on a chair in the dining area, then reaching for Mia, pulled her in a close embrace.

"I owe you a dance," he whispered in her ear.

Mia ran her hands up Kenyon's back over a sweater she knew was cashmere. The heels gave her a height advance when she pressed her cheek to his smooth one. He felt good and smelled even better. Their bodies fit together like interlocking puzzle pieces as she followed his lead.

"You're pretty good at this."

Kenyon pressed a kiss to her ear. "You say that until I step on your pretty shoes."

"You like them?"

He chuckled. "I like the shoes, the skirt *and* the very sexy blouse. I never took you for someone who would go without her underwear."

"I have underwear on, Kenyon."

"Not that I can see."

Mia was wearing underwear, but that was something she wouldn't reveal to him until later. "I hope you haven't eaten, because I put together a little something for dinner."

Kenyon stopped and stared at Mia. "You cooked?"

"No. I ordered from the Kitchen. If I'd known before today that we going to meet tonight I would've tried to prepare something."

"How are the cooking lessons coming?"

"Good. But don't you talk to your mother?"

Spinning her around and around in an intricate step, Kenyon dipped her low, their mouths inches apart. "Of course I talk to her, but not about you. She's never told me who I should or shouldn't date, and she never got into my business when I was with Samantha." He righted her.

"Well, I did talk to your mother about you when I asked her about your favorite dish at the Kitchen."

"What did she say?"

"Meat loaf with a baked potato, wilted spinach and bread pudding with a caramel brandied sauce."

"Yum. What did you order for yourself?"

"Baked chicken, glazed carrots and steamed broccoli." The doorbell echoed loudly. "That must be the food delivery."

"I'll get the door," Kenyon volunteered. Moving over to the intercom, he punched the button, disengaging the lock. Minutes later the delivery clerk handed him two shopping bags, and he gave the young man a generous tip.

"Thank you, Sheriff…I mean, Mr. Chandler."

"That's all right, Jeremy." Whether in uniform or not, everyone in Jonesburg called him Sheriff.

He returned to the dining area to find Mia holding the shopping bag. "What's this?"

"It's a little something for you to open after dinner."

Mia tapped the toe of her right foot. "Aren't you going to give me a hint?"

"Patience, princess."

"Well, you're not the only one with a surprise. I have a little something for you, too." Approaching him with an exaggerated roll of her hips, Mia took the shopping bags from his loose grasp. "I have a bottle of rosé chilling in the fridge. Can you please open it for me? There's a corkscrew on the countertop."

It took less than ten minutes for Mia to transfer the entrées from the disposable containers to the plates at the place settings. She lowered the volume on the CD player, turned up the light in the hanging fixture over the table and allowed Kenyon to seat her before he sat down next to her.

The food was delicious, and Mia wanted to pinch herself because the simple act of sharing a meal with Kenyon was magical. She could be herself without worrying about whether she'd said the wrong thing or say something that would set him off. Men she'd dated in the past seemed intent on challenging everything she said. It was as if they wanted to prove they were more mature, smarter, because she had never been one to dumb down her intelligence.

Tracing the rim of her wineglass with a finger, she stared at the facets on the crystal glass. "I'd asked you to meet me because I needed to tell you something." She went still when Kenyon's fingers grazed the nape of her neck. His hand moved lower inside her blouse collar, kneading the muscles in her shoulder.

Kenyon smiled. Mia's skin felt like velvet under his fingertips. "I'm listening, baby."

"I love you. But that's not all."

It was his turn to freeze. He closed his eyes as his heart pounded a runaway rhythm. "You're pregnant."

A beat passed. "No, Kenyon, I'm not pregnant. I'm using a contraceptive."

"What is it, then?"

"I'm also in love with you. It's something I didn't want or plan, but it just happened."

Pushing back his chair, he eased her over to sit on his lap. "There are times when things happen over which we have no control because it is destined. It was destiny that Xavier married Selena, and it was destiny that brought you to West Virginia."

Resting her head on his shoulder, Mia smiled. "Was it destined that we would fall in love?"

"Of course."

"How presumptuous."

Kenyon kissed her flower-scented hair. "You don't believe in fate?"

"I guess I do."

"Either you do or you don't," he taunted.

"I suppose I do."

"Now that we've gotten that out of the way, what are we going to do now?"

Turning her head, Mia met his eyes that seemed darker and more mysterious in the subdued light. "The ball is in your court, Kenyon. Customarily it's the man who does the asking."

"Are we talking marriage?"

"That is one of my variables."

Kenyon gave the woman in his arms a look that told her what he'd wanted to say the first time they'd made love to each other. "Will you, Mia Eaton, do me the honor of becoming my wife and the mother of our children?"

Wrapping her arms around his neck, she kissed him passionately, her tongue slipping into his mouth. "Yes," she whispered. "Yes, Kenyon Chandler, I will marry you."

"I have to buy you a ring, but right now I can think of a wonderful way to celebrate."

Mia placed her fingers over his lips. "I don't need a ring."

"Yes, you do," he insisted. "Every Eaton woman I saw was wearing an engagement ring, and there's no way my baby isn't going to wear a symbol of our commitment to spend the rest of our lives together. Valentine's Day is next week and we can formally announce our engagement on that day."

"My baby is so romantic," she teased.

"When and where do you want to marry?"

"It will have to be in Dallas. Don't worry about accommodations for your family because I have an uncle on my mom's side who owns a hotel. I'll make certain he'll block out a number of room for out-of-town guests."

"Which month, Mia?"

"Late May or early June, because it gets very hot in Dallas during the summer."

"Have your mother call mine and they can decide what they want. Me, personally I'm going to stay out of the crazy planning nonsense. Just give me the date, time and place and I'll show up."

Mia wanted to ask him if it had been chaotic when he married Samantha, but decided she didn't want to dredge up the ghost of another woman in Kenyon's past life. "Come with me. I have something for you in the bedroom."

Kenyon released Mia. He really wanted to pick her up and carry her into the bedroom, but he didn't want to cause further injury to his arm. He followed her into the bedroom and dissolved in a fit of laughter when he saw black silk boxers on the bed. "You didn't."

Crossing her arms under her breasts, Mia smiled. "Yes I did."

He picked them up and checked the label. "How did you know my size?"

Mia gave him a smug grin. "The night we made love for the first time and I was undressing you, I took a quick glance at the label of your boxer briefs."

"I'll wear them the day we get married. Wait here, and I'll get what I bought for you."

It was Mia's turn to be shocked when she methodically peeled the silver foil paper off the box that contained the most exquisite white silk floor-length nightgown with spaghetti straps and delicate lace trim. She was familiar with the label, and she knew it had set Kenyon back several hundred dollars.

Mia blinked back the tears filling her eyes. "It's beautiful. I'm going to save it for our wedding night."

Kenyon took her in his arms. "I was hoping you'd say that. Speaking of wedding nights, what do you say we get in a little practice before the big event?"

Pressing her breasts to his chest, she cradled his face. "I say yes."

Their gifts lay on a chair while they took their time

undressing each other. Shoes, socks and articles of clothing littered the floor as they fell on the bed. There wasn't time for prolonged foreplay because it had been much too long since they'd made love. Kenyon penetrated Mia with one sure thrust of his hips, the sensation so pleasurable that he feared coming too quickly.

Mouths and hands tasted and charted a journey that they would remember long after the ecstasy faded, and when they reversed positions Mia rode the hardened flesh like a virago under the influence of a powerful drug. She didn't want to stop until the contractions detonated or she passed out from exhaustion. It was the former that was her undoing when Kenyon reversed their positions yet again and pumped his hips until the dam broke, both crying out their awesome climax. They lay joined, savoring the aftermath of a pleasure so exquisite that for wild and rapacious seconds sanity had abandoned them.

Later they left the bed to share a shower, then return to the dining table to clear the dishes and put them in the dishwasher and extinguish the candles and votives. This time when they returned to bed it was to sleep and dream of what lay ahead of them—a destiny with every imaginable happiness.

Epilogue

"I'm not going to cry. I'm not going to cry," Mia whispered over and over as she clutched her father's arm.

Hyman Eaton placed his free hand over his daughter's ice-cold fingers. "Please don't, Mia. You know if you start crying your mother is going start bawling, and I won't be able to deal with her histrionics tonight."

Mia took a deep breath, holding it before she exhaled slowly. "Okay, Daddy."

The ballroom at her uncle's hotel was resplendent with white flowers in every variety ringing the room. She'd chosen Denise Eaton-Fennell as her only attendant because most of her female cousins were either pregnant or breastfeeding. Kenyon had chosen Billie Lord—or William, as he'd introduced himself to her family—as his best man. The restaurateur appeared uncomfortable in his cutaway suit, claiming the last time he looked like a penguin was at his own wedding.

Letitia and Sylvia had conferred by telephone for several months before Kenyon's mother flew to Dallas to meet the mother of the bride in person. Letitia was miffed that Mia had purchased her wedding gown in Virginia, but she had to agree the dress was incomparable when it arrived.

Mia and Kenyon had driven to an exclusive bridal shop in Alexandria, Virginia, to look at gowns. She selected the third one she'd tried on. The fact that it was a Vera Wang creation was like finding a rare diamond. It was a simple strapless gown with a seeded pearl bodice and low draped back with gathered fabric fashioned into a rose. Her headdress was a small pillbox hat with a detachable veil.

The elaborate ceremony was the wedding of the season, with a six-course sit-down dinner, an orchestra, a jazz band and a DJ. The only thing missing was a gospel choir.

She and Kenyon were going to honeymoon for a week in Cabo San Lucas before returning to Jonesburg. Dr. Lyman had advertised and hired a part-time physician assistant to fill in for Mia while she was away. However, Mia knew the assistant's hours would increase as Dr. Lyman's arthritis progressed.

Mia thought her father looked exceedingly handsome in his tuxedo. He bonded with his son-in-law over poker, imported cigars and bourbon in the days before the wedding. She wanted to tell Hyman Eaton that Kenyon wasn't much of a drinker, but then changed her mind. Kenyon was old enough to know when he'd had enough. She'd waited for him to come to bed hungover, but it never happened. It was apparent her man knew his limit.

Cradling a bouquet of pink and white roses, Mia pulled back her hair to reveal her bare shoulders. The diamond necklace around her neck competed with the brilliance of the stones in her earlobes. The necklace had belonged to her grandmother and was something old. Her gown was something new, and the garter around her thigh was something blue. The music changed and the strains of the "Wedding March" floated through the closed doors to the ballroom.

Hyman patted his daughter's hand. "Are you ready, baby girl?"

"Yes, Daddy." And she was. She was ready to become Mrs. Kenyon Chandler.

Hyman nodded to the two young men standing at the doors. "Open them, please."

A gasp escaped those assembled as they rose to acknowledge the bride on her father's arm. He led her slowly down the white-carpeted aisle to where the groom stood with his best man opposite the matron of honor. Denise's pink silk gown matched the flowers in the bridal bouquet.

A smile was on Mia's lips as she nodded to the Eatons, ranging from middle age to infancy, then she turned her happy smile on the Yateses and finally her in-laws. Letitia and Hyman had invited the West Virginians to their home the following day for an authentic Texas cookout complete with barbecue ribs, aged rib eye steaks and the fixings.

Mia focused her attention on the man who in a matter of minutes would become her husband. He was breathtakingly gorgeous in his formal attire, the gray waistcoat an exact match for his incredible eyes.

The appellate judge, one of Hyman's golfing buddies, had volunteered to officiate. He adjusted his black robe, then cleared his voice. "Who gives this woman in marriage?"

Hyman bit his lip and inhaled. He'd cautioned Mia about becoming emotional, and for a nanosecond he couldn't find his voice. "I do," he said amid murmurs